Beneath Missouri Stars

a quilting cozy

Carol Dean Jones

C&T PUBLISHING
Another Maker Inspired!

Publisher: Amy Barrett-Daffin

Creative Director / Technical Editor:
Gailen Runge

Acquisitions Editor: Roxane Cerda

Managing Editor: Liz Aneloski

Project Writer: Teresa Stroin

Cover/Book Designer: April Mostek

Production Coordinator:
Zinnia Heinzmann

Production Editor: Alice Mace Nakanishi

Illustrator: Kirstie L. Pettersen

Photo Assistant: Gregory Ligman

Cover photography by Estefany Gonzalez
of C&T Publishing, Inc.

Cover quilt: *Beneath Missouri Stars*, 2019,
by the author

Published by C&T Publishing, Inc.,
P.O. Box 1456, Lafayette, CA 94549

Library of Congress Cataloging-in-
Publication Data

Names: Jones, Carol Dean, author.

Title: Beneath Missouri stars /
Carol Dean Jones.

Description: Lafayette, CA :
C&T Publishing, [2020] | Series:
Quilting cozy series ; book 11

Identifiers: LCCN 2019051309 |
ISBN 9781617459955 (trade paperback) |
ISBN 9781617459962 (ebook)

Subjects: GSAFD: Mystery fiction.

Classification: LCC PS3610.O6224 B46
2020 | DDC 813/.6--dc23

LC record available at
https://lccn.loc.gov/2019051309

POD Edition

A Quilting Cozy Series

by Carol Dean Jones

Tie Died (book 1)

Running Stitches (book 2)

Sea Bound (book 3)

Patchwork Connections (book 4)

Stitched Together (book 5)

Moon Over the Mountain (book 6)

The Rescue Quilt (book 7)

Missing Memories (book 8)

Tattered & Torn (book 9)

Left Holding the Bag (book 10)

Beneath Missouri Stars (book 11)

Frayed Edges (book 12)

Dedicated to Caterina

Acknowledgments

I want to acknowledge three special friends who have patiently read and reread the many drafts that ultimately resulted in this book. Despite my creator's resistance, they helped me see the need for certain changes that turned out to be needed in every case. Therefore, special thanks go to Jo Windle, Janice Packard, and Joyce Frazier, three amazing women and forever friends.

I also want to thank C&T Publishing for the willingness to take a chance on me, and especially the entire staff who worked tirelessly to get the first ten books of this series published. The team's decision to add the patterns for the feature quilts has been well received, as evidenced by the many expressions of gratitude I've received from readers.

Special thanks go to my many loyal readers who have kept me writing with their frequent blog comments and positive emails encouraging me to keep the series going.

Chapter 1

"I hope you don't have plans for Friday," Sarah announced excitedly as she hurried into her friend's kitchen. "You and I are going to see Austin Bailey live in concert."

Sarah was surprised when her usually exuberant friend didn't respond. The country singer was from Sophie's hometown, and over the last decade he had become extremely popular, especially with Sophie. But instead of showing any enthusiasm, Sophie simply continued dishing up freshly baked cinnamon buns.

"Coffee's on," Sophie announced.

"Sophie? Did you hear what I said?"

Sophie didn't respond right away but finally turned toward her good friend and said, "Sarah, I'm sorry to disappoint you, but I really don't want to go. Those concert halls are so crowded and loud. That's for the young folks. And besides," she added, "we'd probably be sitting way up in the nosebleed section, and with my hip …"

"No, Sophie," Sarah responded excitedly. "We won't be going to the concert hall. He's doing a private concert right here in the Village."

Sophie looked at her friend skeptically. "A world-famous country music singer performing here in our retirement community? I don't think so …"

Sophie—short, rotund, and always ready with a wisecrack—sat down quietly and began eating the first of the two buns she had placed on her plate. "Sit down, Sarah," she said, still seeming to be uninterested in her friend's announcement. "Get a cinnamon bun while they're hot." But after a few moments, she gave in to her curiosity and without looking up said, "So go ahead with this Austin Bailey nonsense. What are you talking about?"

"It's not nonsense, Sophie. I had a call from the volunteer coordinator at the nursing home, and he's scheduled a private concert just for the residents, the staff, and the volunteers. They're keeping it quiet, especially from the press, so you can't tell anyone."

"No one would believe me if I did," Sophie said, obviously beginning to warm up to the idea. "And I'm not sure I believe it myself," she added. "Isn't he on tour back East?"

"I heard he returned home when someone in his family died, but I don't know why he's here in Middletown or why he's doing this private concert. All I know is that we're invited, and that's actually all I care about. Charles thinks I'm being silly, but I'm practically giddy about seeing Austin," she said, trying not to giggle. "We might even get to meet him," she added with a twinkle in her eye.

"Oh, so now it's 'Austin,' is it?" Sophie teased, a tinge of her usual playfulness returning. "But seriously, how come I'm invited? I'm not a volunteer, and I'm sure not a nursing home resident, at least not yet."

"The volunteers can bring one guest each, and Charles said he thought you'd enjoy it more than he would," Sarah replied, ignoring her friend's sardonic comment and tone. "Sophie, please come …"

"Oh," Sophie answered reluctantly, "I don't know …"

Sarah took a bite out of her cinnamon bun as Sophie polished off her second one and reached for another. Sarah knew Sophie loved country music and especially Austin Bailey. "Seriously, Sophie, what's going on? I thought you'd be thrilled at the chance to see him in person, and especially in such a private setting."

Sophie didn't answer right away but finally sighed and pushed her plate aside. "Austin Bailey was the performer at the last concert that my husband, Cliff, and I attended together. We were in St. Louis on our second honeymoon … or was it our third?" she mused with a deep frown. "Maybe it was …"

"Go ahead, Sophie," Sarah interrupted impatiently. "Tell me about the concert."

"There's nothing in particular to tell," she responded. "It's just that we had a fantastic time and Cliff was so excited about Austin. You see, he knew Austin's father when they were young, and he knew how proud Mr. Bailey would have been if he had lived. Cliff said, 'That young man will be a star someday,' and he was right."

Sarah sat quietly, realizing that Sophie had more to say.

"A year later Cliff was in the nursing home, and not long after that he was gone. I'll never forget that concert, though," Sophie added with a faraway smile. She sighed and continued, "It just seems strange that he'll be performing right where Cliff died. I just wish …"

Sarah reached across the table and squeezed Sophie's hand, knowing that this was one of those rare times her friend would express her hidden emotions. She was always ready with the jokes and her infectious cackle but avoided displaying her grief.

"Oh, I'm fine," Sophie remarked, pulling her hand back and dismissing her friend's concern. "More coffee?"

"I'll get it," Sarah replied as she stood and headed for the coffeepot. Glancing out the window, she saw the townhouse across the street that had been her first home when she had moved to Cunningham Village several years ago. Sophie had taken her under her wing, and they had become fast friends. However, Sarah rarely got a glimpse of the pain her friend carried just beneath the surface of her boisterous and jovial personality.

Sarah carried the coffeepot back to the table and refilled their mugs.

At that moment, there was a frantic scratching at the back door. "Since you're up," Sophie said, "you might as well let those two little rascals in."

Moments later, Barney and Emma came bounding across the kitchen floor, heading for Sophie and licking their lips excitedly. They both knew an easy mark when they saw one. Sarah never gave table scraps to her Barney, but she had given up long ago trying to stop Sophie from feeding him from the table. Emma, Sophie's lovable rescue, was taking on the shape of her owner, rounded through the middle.

By the time Sarah sat back down, both dogs were curled up on Emma's blanket devouring leftover cinnamon buns.

"So what do you think about the concert? Will you be my date?" Sarah asked cautiously.

"I will be accompanying you," Sophie stated with resolve. "But seriously, I'm still curious about why he's doing a private concert here. Why here?"

"I'll nose around a little and see what I can find out."

* * * * *

As she was walking home with Barney at her side, Sarah passed the community center and nursing home complex, which sat beyond a manicured green space where residents and visitors were sitting on benches enjoying the early morning sun. It was only a couple more blocks to the home she and Charles had built after they got married, but, on a whim, she decided to turn around and see if Vicky, the volunteer coordinator at the nursing home, was available.

Cunningham Village was a complete retirement community offering individual homes like she and Charles owned, one-story townhomes like Sophie's, and the nursing home and rehab center. Also, there were apartments that offered various levels of care and an incredible community center.

Sarah had originally been very reluctant to move to a retirement community. After her husband died, she had felt lonely living in the home where she had raised her children, but she had her memories and especially loved the garden Jonathan had helped her create. But her daughter, Martha, and son, Jason, had been insistent, saying that she couldn't manage the large house forever, and they felt it was a good time to make the move.

Now, several years later, she had to agree that it had been an excellent decision. She had made many friends, learned to quilt, and met the man she ultimately married.

"Life is good," she said to Barney as they strolled toward the building.

"Sarah and Barney," Vicky exclaimed. "Good to see you both. Come on in. I'll be with you in just a moment." She jotted a few words on the paper in front of her, slid it into a file folder, and set it aside. "So, coffee, Sarah? I just made a fresh pot."

"I'm coffeed out, Vicky, but thank you. Barney and I just left Sophie's house …"

"Okay, so that means you probably don't want one of these donuts either," Vicky said with a chuckle. Barney's ears perked up.

"You're right," Sarah responded. "It was cinnamon bun day at Sophie's house. I've reached my target sugar level."

Vicky swiveled her chair around, reached into the supply cabinet behind her, and pulled out a large mason jar. Barney's tail began to wag. "I'll bet there's one thing that won't be refused," she said as she took out two bone-shaped biscuits. Barney looked pleadingly at Sarah, who nodded her approval, and he hurried over to get them from Vicky.

While Barney lay in the corner munching the biscuits, Sarah and Vicky discussed Sarah's latest visit with Sonya Lang, the 96-year-old patient whom she visited weekly. "Sonya asks the nurse every morning if it's the day you visit, and she shows off the quilt you made for her to everyone. You've given her something to look forward to."

"I wonder if I should start seeing her more often," Sarah said, considering the implications as she said it. She already visited a second resident every week, had the quilt club every Tuesday, and taught an introductory quilting class at Ruth's quilt shop, and Charles liked for her to go with him to the gym occasionally. *I probably have enough on my plate as it is*, she pondered. "Anyway," she continued aloud, "I was wondering what you could tell me about Austin Bailey's visit here. It seems strange that he'd agree to perform in such a small venue."

"Well, I guess I can tell you, Sarah, but this is strictly confidential. We've had to keep what I'm about to tell you under wraps for nearly a year now. If the press were to get ahold of this …"

"Don't worry, Vicky. My lips are sealed, but I must admit that I'm very curious."

"Well," Vicky continued, "last October, Austin's sister brought their grandmother here for care. It was done very secretively."

"And she's still here?" Sarah exclaimed, looking stunned.

"No, she passed a few weeks ago," Vicky said regretfully.

"Oh, I'm so sorry," Sarah sympathized. Barney, noting the change in her voice, looked up at her for a moment, but returned to his biscuits. "That explains why Austin cut his latest tour short," she added thoughtfully. "How were you able to keep all this quiet? He's so famous."

"Well, first of all," Vicky explained, "she was his grandmother on his mother's side, so the names were different. She was a Henderson. Austin's sister, who is married and lives several hours from here in Missouri, is a Dodson, so there was no way anyone here would have made the connection."

"Austin never visited?"

"No, and he very much regrets that now, but he didn't want there to be any publicity that might upset his grandmother. He loved her very much, and I'm sure it was hard for him to stay away, but he did it for her. He called here every week and talked to her and the nurses, but he said he was her nephew and used a fake name. No one ever suspected."

"That must have been hard for him," Sarah said sadly.

"It was. His grandmother had raised him after his parents were killed in an automobile accident when he and his sister were very young. He told me once that she's the one who encouraged his music career."

"You've talked to him?" Sarah asked with surprise.

Vicky laughed. "I sure have, Sarah, and he's a very nice young man. You'll love him when you meet him."

"I'll meet him?"

"You will," Vicky responded. "He specifically requested that you be at the concert so he could meet you."

"Me?" Sarah exclaimed, looking confused. "Why me?"

"Because he wants to thank you for your kindness to his grandmother."

"I met her?"

"Yes. Remember the woman who wanted to see your quilts, and you brought four or five to her room back in the spring?"

"Yes, but that wasn't a Henderson. Her name was Browning."

"You're right, but Ruth Henderson was across the hall and you …"

"Oh, I remember. I saw her peering out trying to see the quilts, and I took them over for her to see. That was Austin Bailey's grandmother? I remember she was very frail."

"Yes, but she remembered you and told her grandson about the quilts when he called her. He thought it was very nice of you to spend time with her. You went back a couple of times, didn't you?"

"I stopped in to say hello occasionally when I visited Mrs. Browning, but one day she wasn't there anymore."

"Yes, she got transferred to the Memory Care Unit a few months later. Sad story."

They sat quietly for a few moments. Barney, sensing the change in Sarah's mood, got up and moved to her side and laid his head on her lap. Sarah gently scratched his ear.

"So now I know about his connection to the nursing home, but the concert?"

"I think it's his way of saying thank you to the staff and volunteers. As I said, he's a fine young man, kind and caring."

Sarah didn't want to take up any more of Vicky's time, so she hooked Barney's leash onto his collar and stood to leave as they said their goodbyes. "Thank you, Vicky, for sharing this with me. I'm looking forward to the concert and meeting this young man. Oh, and by the way, Charles said I could give his place to Sophie. I hope that's okay."

"Absolutely. Sophie volunteered here for several years after her husband died. Just make sure she understands the need for secrecy. It could be a disaster if this were to become public knowledge."

But as it turned out, there was no way to keep it quiet.

Chapter 2

"I think almost everyone is here," Ruth, owner of the Running Stitches quilt shop, said as she looked at the group of Tuesday Night Quilters crowded around the work-table in the back of her quilt shop. Some had already pulled out handwork and were beginning to stitch as they chatted with their friends.

"Allison is on her way," Ruth's sister, Anna, announced as she entered the workroom. "She just called to say that her husband got home late, but she's leaving now."

"Sophie, you look particularly happy tonight. What's going on?" Ruth asked, noticing that their newest member was giggling like a teenager.

"Oh, I'm just so excited about …" she started to respond, before Sarah poked her in the ribs. "Oh, I forgot," she said to Sarah and, turning to Ruth, she added, "It's just something I was thinking about. Sorry." Looking contrite, she continued, "Please go on with the meeting."

"I'd like to begin by introducing our guest," Ruth said, turning to the woman who was sitting near the table. "This is Monica Friedman. Monica is a friend of mine, and she has made an interesting request. Monica, as you may know, is the coordinator of the Meals on Wheels program here in Middletown. Is everyone familiar with the program?"

"I've heard people talk about it, but I don't know exactly what it is," Caitlyn responded. At seventeen, Caitlyn was the group's youngest member and was quickly becoming a talented quilter. "They take meals to old people, don't they?"

Ruth smiled and said, "Yes, they take meals to home-bound people who are unable to prepare their own meals. Monica, would you tell us a little about the program? Then we can talk about your request."

Ruth stepped aside and Monica, a woman who appeared to be in her mid-fifties, took her place at the head of the table. Glancing around at the members, she was surprised by the wide range of ages. The young woman who had spoken appeared to be the youngest, and the others represented a variety of ages, including several elderly women. She was surprised to see a young man in the group. Obviously, they all had quilting in common, and all appeared eager to hear what she had to say.

"I'd like to start by giving you just a quick history of Meals on Wheels, and what we do. We're a nonprofit organization, and our goal is to help homebound people to eat well and remain in their own homes as long as possible. The hot meals are planned by registered dieticians and are designed to meet at least one-third of an elderly person's daily nutritional needs. They are delivered primarily by volunteers who can also provide a quick safety check, since our clients are usually alone and isolated. Sometimes that volunteer is the only human contact the person has.

"This program," she continued, "was originally developed in England following World War II and spread to this country during the 60s and 70s. I don't want to turn this into a lecture, so let me stop here and see if there are any questions about the program."

"I have one," Delores responded. "Who pays for these meals?"

"It varies. In some communities, the recipients make a small contribution depending on their circumstances, but the program is funded by private donations and by grants from the government, private corporations, and foundations."

"Do they only get one meal a day?" Caitlyn asked, obviously very interested in the program. Sarah knew that Caitlyn often expressed interest in becoming a social worker and working with the elderly, and that she would find this program particularly interesting. Sarah glanced at Sophie, who was smiling, clearly thinking the same thing.

Monica explained that there was only one delivery a day, but the volunteers brought one hot meal at lunchtime and a deli meal for the evening.

"Do the volunteers stay and visit?"

"That's up to the volunteers and their schedules. Since they usually have other meals to deliver, they can't stay long, but they certainly stay long enough for a little conversation. They develop a relationship with the people they serve, and that brings me to the reason I'm here," she said, turning to Ruth.

Ruth stood and joined Monica at the front of the room. "Monica asked me if I thought this group might be willing to make placemats that the volunteers could take to their clients. We were thinking perhaps something colorful that would brighten their days. We could stick with simple patterns, and since we always use cotton, they would be durable and washable. What do you think?"

There was growing chatter around the table. The club members were not only agreeing to the idea but already talking about potential designs. Laughing, Ruth said, "Well, it looks to me like this idea is a hit." Turning to Monica, she asked, "When would you like to have them?"

"The holidays will be coming up in a few months," Monica said, "and we were hoping to deliver them around Thanksgiving and Christmas."

"That gives us plenty of time," Ruth concluded. "Right?" she added, looking around the room. Everyone agreed.

"But we need to know how many you need," Delores said.

"We currently serve 103 people in this district, but that number changes. I would say we could take as many as you folks want to make. If we get more than we need, we'll save them for new people who come into the program."

Ruth suggested they break for refreshments, which she had set up on a side table, and continue to discuss the project. Monica stayed for another half hour and talked with the quilters, all of whom had their own questions about the program and stories to share.

After Monica left and the quilters had reassembled around the worktable, Ruth asked, "Okay, when would you like to get together and begin this project?"

"We don't have anything else on our agenda right now," Christina said. "Why don't we start planning tonight?"

"Good idea," Sarah responded, "and I think we should begin by deciding what size we want the placemats to be. Then we can all just start making them, as many as we are each able to do."

"Will we be working on these at our meetings or at home?" Caitlyn asked. Caitlyn was leaving for college in a few weeks but clearly wanted to be included in the project. "I won't have much time, but I'd like to make a few at least."

"I think we can work on them here and at home," Ruth responded. "Whatever works for each of us."

"Do we have any money in our club account that could cover some of the fabric?" Allison asked. Allison had slipped in while Monica was talking and had quietly pulled a chair up to the table next to Caitlyn.

"We have $150 left that could go for new fabric, but you probably have enough scraps in your stash to get started. And don't forget about the baskets of scraps we have in the back room. Let's pull those out tonight and see what we have that's bright and cheerful."

Caitlyn and Allison, the two youngest and most energetic members, hopped up and headed for the storage room. They came out dragging three large baskets filled to the brim with scraps from past projects and the ends of bolts that Ruth had tossed in.

"Someone needs to organize this mess," Sophie announced as she pulled out a few pieces and laid them aside.

"Someone needs to do that at my house too," Becky responded with a chuckle. Becky had just joined the group after taking Sarah's Introduction to Quilting class. She was a skilled seamstress and had been sewing since she was in high school but had never learned to quilt. She became interested during her first visit to Ruth's shop when she saw the beautiful quilts hanging on the walls.

"I was reading a quilter's blog the other night," Anna stated, "and she was talking about how she deals with the fabric that is left over when she finishes a project."

"I have a huge basket spilling over with exactly that," Christina interjected. "I don't even know why I keep it. I can never find what I want because it's such a tangled-up mess."

"Well, what this quilter does is she cuts it all into two-and-a-half-inch strips or five-inch squares, depending on the size of her leftover pieces."

"All of it?" Sophie asked with a frown.

"No, just the pieces that are less than a yard. She keeps the bigger pieces and stores them by color."

"I like the idea of the five-inch squares," Christina commented. "When I make scrap quilts, I will sometimes buy them packaged as charm packs in order to get lots of variety. It would be great to already have my own pre-cuts." Turning to Peggy, she added, "You made that blue and yellow quilt of yours with charm packs you bought here at the shop, didn't you, Peggy?"

"Yes," Peggy responded, looking away. Peggy, a woman who appeared to be in her early seventies, didn't attend the group regularly and no one knew exactly why. She would occasionally appear, saying she was sorry to have missed so many meetings, but she never offered an explanation. Once when Peggy reached across the table for something her shirt slipped up a few inches in the back and Sarah saw an ugly bruise. It made her wonder, but, of course, she said nothing.

"I've heard that some clubs have five-inch square exchanges," Sarah added. "It's a great way to build variety into your stash."

"And you make whole quilts with these little squares?" Caitlyn asked, looking doubtful.

"Yes, or you can cut them in half lengthwise and have rectangles, or you can use them to make half-square triangles, Hourglass blocks, Pinwheels. It's a very handy size to have cut and ready to use."

"Okay, back to this project," Delores said, attempting to get the group back on track. "I recommend that we make these placemats as close to 12″ by 18″ as possible. You could design six simple six-inch blocks and place them two down and three across, or you could just do diagonal stripes or simple squares—whatever you want to do. It's a chance to be creative and try out some of the techniques you've wanted to experiment with."

"We could also use stray blocks left over from other projects," Ruth suggested. "I have a drawer full of orphan blocks that I knew would come in handy someday."

"I have a suggestion for finishing them," Sarah announced. "I think we should just stack the finished top and the back with the batting and turn them instead of binding them. That way, with an outline stitch along the outside edge, it will hold up better in the wash."

"And be a lot faster to make," someone added with a chuckle.

"I don't know how to do that," Caitlyn said, looking worried.

"Neither do I," Allison added.

"Let's just concentrate on making the tops for now," Ruth responded. "We can set a meeting aside for finishing them off with backs and batting."

"I'm going to get started on mine just as soon as I get home," Sophie announced.

For someone who fought the idea of learning to quilt, my friend has sure jumped in with both feet, Sarah thought with a smile.

"On the notions rack I have several books of patterns that use scraps. Feel free to look through them for ideas," Ruth said.

"And there are hundreds of placemat patterns online," Anna suggested.

"What about the quilting?" Caitlyn asked, obviously beginning to feel overwhelmed. Sarah and Sophie knew it wasn't the project that was getting to her. Caitlyn was scheduled to leave for California in a few weeks, where she'd be living with an elderly distant cousin she'd never met and attending college nearby. She'd been determined to make a big adventure of going away to school, but as the day to leave grew closer, she was becoming increasingly anxious about leaving her father and the friends who had become family to her.

"We could do straight-line machine quilting to hold it together, couldn't we?" someone suggested.

"We could," Ruth responded. "Just go ahead and make your tops, and we'll deal with the quilting later, okay?" Caitlyn nodded her agreement but looked worried, knowing that her time was limited.

Sarah leaned over close to the young girl and whispered, "Come over this week, and we'll make some together." Caitlyn let out a deep sigh of relief and mouthed 'thank you' to her friend.

Chapter 3

Friday afternoon had finally arrived. Sophie reached for Sarah's hand and squeezed it as she leaned over and whispered, "This is the most exciting thing I've done in years. Thank you for including me."

Sarah smiled at her friend and replied, "Me too. Well, except for marrying Charles. That was exciting. Oh, and honeymooning in Paris. That was pretty exciting, too," she added with a youthful giggle that Sophie often told her was not befitting a seventy-something-year-old woman. Until she met Charles, she didn't think she had giggled since she was a teenager. *He just brings it out in me*, she thought with a smile.

All the tables had been removed from the nursing home cafeteria and replaced with folding chairs for the residents, staff, and volunteers, with lots of interspersed space for wheelchairs, which were being wheeled in as Sarah and Sophie waited. They had arrived early, determined to have front-row seats.

Sarah looked around to see if Sonya was attending, but didn't see her. She knew Sonya was probably too frail. Just then, she spotted the other patient she visited, Nadine Browning, as an aide was wheeling her into the room. She got Nadine's attention and motioned for her to join them in the front. Nadine grinned excitedly and appeared to be pointing her aide in their direction.

"This is taking forever," Sophie complained, noticing that patients were still being brought in.

"It takes a long time to get us old folks up and out of our rooms," Nadine commented as her aide positioned her wheelchair next to the two women. Sarah had been visiting Nadine for the past five or six weeks and found it to be one the most enjoyable assignments she'd had since joining the volunteer staff. Nadine was eighty-eight years old and reported that she had been very active until she fell and broke her hip the previous winter.

According to Nadine, all her troubles started with that fall. She had a hip replacement and came to the Rehab Unit of the nursing home for physical therapy, but while there she suffered a stroke, which, according to Nadine, left her with physical limitations, including the inability to walk. "It was going to require more physical therapy," she said, "and since I had been living alone in an apartment in town, my doctor didn't think I should go home."

Nadine, with no family to turn to, decided to stay in the nursing home, at least while she was getting physical therapy. Fortunately, she had long-term care insurance and savings that made it financially possible. She hoped to move to an assisted living unit within the next few months. "We'll be neighbors," Sarah had said excitedly when they first talked about it.

What Sarah appreciated about Nadine was her positive attitude and cheerful disposition. Sarah was frequently assigned as a visitor to patients with no family who were isolated, alone, and depressed. Nadine was one of the few she could count on to meet her visits with a smile. Nadine was fascinated with Sarah's quilting and encouraged her to bring whatever she was working on when she came to visit.

"You know," Nadine commented, "I saw Austin Bailey in person several years ago when he was in St. Louis. I think it was about ten years ago …"

"His Homecoming Tour?" Sophie asked eagerly, leaning across Sarah.

"Yes!" Nadine answered excitedly. "You heard about that tour?"

"Heard about it!" Sophie exclaimed. "I was there. It was exactly twelve years ago this month. Austin had been playing small towns around the country for a year or so, and he wanted to go back to Missouri, where his family was. My husband was alive then and we drove to St. Louis and stayed over for a few days." Sophie's eyes sparkled as she reminisced. Sarah wished she'd known Sophie during those days.

"That's quite a coincidence," Nadine added. "He wasn't that popular yet."

"I know, but my husband predicted that he would be," Sophie announced with a proprietary grin.

"Imagine that," Nadine mused. "You and I were sitting in the same room back then listening to Austin Bailey, and here we are now, years later. It's a small world," she added, shaking her head. Sophie and Nadine began chatting like old friends, and Sarah excused herself to go speak with one of the nurses.

Turning to Nadine, Sophie asked, "Aren't you the person who just start using a laptop to visit with your out-of-town friends?"

Nadine excitedly clapped her hands and said, "Oh my, have I ever—and it's such fun! I'm on this social media site, and I'm in touch with two of my classmates from high school every day. We have at least seventy years to catch up on," she added with a chuckle.

"How did you learn to use those sites?" Sophie asked. "There are a couple of old girlfriends I'd love to catch up with."

"Simple," Nadine responded. "My nurse's son taught me. The kids know all about that stuff. At first it was pretty confusing, but I finally started to catch on."

Sophie had been wondering about social media herself lately, since it seemed that the rest of the world was leaving her behind. She thought about her grandchild, Penny, and wondered if Penny could help her.

Sophie had been reluctant to get involved with the new technology, but her friend Norman had insisted that she get a smartphone so they could text, and she had to admit she was enjoying it. "Perhaps I need a laptop," she said aloud as she made the decision to talk with Norman and Penny about it.

"Speaking of confusion," Sophie said as Sarah returned to her seat. "What's all that noise behind the stage, and why haven't we seen Austin Bailey yet? This thing was supposed to start a half hour ago. I knew this was too good to be true …"

Sarah slipped into her seat, and at that moment a man whom she recognized as the nursing home administrator walked out on the stage and over to the microphone that had been set up for Austin Bailey. He tapped it a few times.

"Can you hear me?" he asked as his blaring voice reverberated off the walls.

"What?" someone yelled from the back, and several people chuckled.

"Jim isn't wearing his hearing aid again," Nadine snickered.

"Okay, I have an announcement," the man began.

"See?" Sophie announced self-righteously. "What did I tell you? Too good to be true. He isn't going to be here."

"Austin Bailey," the man continued, "has been detained. I've been told he'll be with us within the hour, so, in the meantime, our staff is serving coffee and tea at the back of the room. The nursing staff will assist those unable to get back there. Please stay with us. This promises to be a most entertaining evening."

Sarah smiled at Sophie and said, "See? Everything is just running a bit late."

A moment later she gasped as she realized there were uniformed police stationed at every exit.

* * * * *

"Charles, have you heard anything?" Sarah had slipped her cell phone out of her pocket and called her husband at home.

"What do you mean? About what?" Charles asked.

"We appear to be on lockdown over here," she responded. "The show has been delayed, and there are police at every exit."

"What makes you think you're on lockdown?" Charles asked, assuming his wife was overdramatizing the situation.

"One man attempted to leave, and he was sent back to his seat."

"Maybe he was a resident," Charles surmised. "Sarah, I doubt …"

"No, he was dressed in a suit and tie. He was obviously one of the visitors or maybe a volunteer. Can you see anything from the front window?"

"No, but I'll walk over to the nursing home and see what I can find out."

"Take your cell phone. I don't think they'll let you in."

"We'll see about that," he remarked with irritation. Sarah knew not to take it personally. Charles was a retired detective and assumed certain privileges that the younger generation of cops didn't necessarily agree with.

Ten minutes later the phone quacked, her signal that Charles was calling. Sophie snickered as she always did when Charles called. "Your pocket is quacking," she announced.

Sarah answered the phone with, "Well?"

"I can't find out a thing. I don't know any of these young cops. Things are changing so fast in that department, and I just …"

"Charles, stop," his wife said, interrupting what she knew could become a tirade about all the changes since what he remembered as the good old days in the department. "What's happening out there?"

"Well, there's an ambulance, but the emergency personnel are inside the building, and the driver isn't talking. The stretcher isn't in the back, so I assume whatever's going on in there required a stretcher. The medical examiner's car is here too, but it's empty. That's not a particularly good sign. There's just no one to ask who's willing to talk to me. One kid in uniform who I tried to talk to responded with,

'You old folks need to move on back behind the tape.' I felt like smacking him," he grumbled.

"Please don't smack anyone, Charles. There are enough cops here to drag you off to jail. Just call me if you learn anything. Can't you talk to someone at the station?"

Charles' lieutenant and close friend had died the past year, leaving him few contacts in the department. "With Matt gone and Hal out of town, there really isn't anyone around anymore to grant me special favors, Sarah. We'll just have to wait. How are they treating you and Sophie?"

"Oh, there's no problem. They're walking around serving coffee and cookies, and the administrator said Austin plans to go on within the hour. I just can't imagine …" but then Sarah stopped talking.

"Sarah? Are you still there?" Charles asked when the line suddenly became quiet.

After a few moments, his wife spoke, saying, "Hold on, Charles. … Okay, he just came out. I'll leave the line open, and maybe you can hear what he has to say."

"Wait, who just came out? Austin?" Charles asked.

"No, Jeff Holbrooke, the administrator," she responded. "Hang on."

"Okay, folks," Holbrooke begin. "I'm sorry for the delay and all the confusion. I'm sure you're aware of the police presence, and I want to explain." An anxious buzz filled the room.

Raising both arms, he added, "Please hold it down. Even with the microphone, I can't talk above all this." The noise began to diminish until the room finally became hushed as everyone waited for Holbrooke to speak.

"As I was saying," he continued, "we regret the delay. In the meantime, I have some sad news to report. The young woman, Angela Padilla, who was scheduled to join Mr. Bailey on stage, has had an accident and won't be appearing. Mr. Bailey, although distraught, assures me he plans to go on with the performance but requests your indulgence. He needs a little time. Since it's approaching time for the evening meal, the staff will begin passing out sandwiches to anyone interested, residents and visitors included. Thank you." He walked off the stage, ignoring the barrage of questions that followed him.

The room continued to buzz as everyone speculated about what might have happened.

Charles, on the other hand, was not speculating. He was watching the paramedics solemnly carrying the stretcher back toward the ambulance. The black body bag was zipped closed.

Chapter 4

As it turned out, Austin Bailey was unable to perform. The police released all the residents, and they were returned to their rooms. The officers then systematically spoke with the guests, spending more time with those sitting in the front rows and to the right side of the room near the makeshift dressing room.

It wasn't until the next morning's newspaper came out that everyone learned that the young woman had died in Austin's dressing room. According to the article, the medical examiner had not yet been able to determine the cause of death. "They're just not ready to announce it," Charles had said earlier.

Sarah had scanned the article once at home and was now sitting at Sophie's kitchen table reading the entire article more carefully. "Did you see this?" she called to Sophie, who was standing just outside the kitchen door waiting for Emma. "The girl was in her early twenties and had been singing with Austin off and on for the past several years."

"I saw that," Sophie called. "Farther on down it says she was the daughter of a good friend of his. I wonder what happened to her. There's no mention of foul play."

"Hal called Charles late last night from Florida, where he was visiting his sister. The department wants him to cut his vacation short and return to work because of the potential publicity." Hal was a young detective who had worked with Charles on a previous case and was one of the only members of the department that Charles had any connection with. He and Hal had both been close friends with Matt, Charles' previous lieutenant who had died the year before.

"Did Hal know any more than what's in the paper?" Sophie was now wiping Emma's feet before letting her back into the kitchen. If there was a mud puddle anywhere in the yard, Emma could always be counted on to drag her beautiful cream-colored coat through it.

"He just filled Charles in on some of the details."

"And?"

"He said that the Padilla girl sang with Austin occasionally but that for the past few months she'd been working as a nursing assistant at the nursing home."

"That's strange. The article said that she lived in Missouri. I wonder why she was working here," Sophie mused. "What else did he say? Do they know what happened to her?"

"They won't know much about her death until they get the medical examiner's report," Sarah responded.

"Well, it's early," Sophie grunted as she hung onto the door frame to pull herself up the small step and into the kitchen.

"Have you had that hip looked at yet?"

"Soon, Sarah. Soon. Stop nagging and tell me what else Hal and Charles had to say."

"Mainly Charles, and probably Hal, is saying that you and I are to stay out of it."

"Of course. Why would we get involved? We don't know any of these people." Sophie looked at Sarah as she spoke with a wide-eyed look of innocence.

"Don't give me that," Sarah disputed. "I'll bet you already have your 3″ by 5″ card file box out and labeled. But really, this time the police are investigating, and it really doesn't involve any of us."

"True," Sophie acceded, but without conviction.

"That tone of voice concerns me, Sophie. This has nothing whatsoever to do with us."

"That's not exactly true, Sarah. Austin was from my hometown, you know …"

"Yes, but he's a good forty years younger than you and wasn't even born when you moved away."

"True, but it's a connection …"

"Sophie, stop. We are *not* getting involved."

"Absolutely not," Sophie responded, again wide-eyed. She was still trying to pull off her look of innocence but without much success.

"So," Sarah said, changing the subject. "I told Caitlyn I'd help her with her placemats today. She's coming to my house for lunch, and we'll be sewing all afternoon. Do you want to join us?"

Sophie's face lit up as she thought about it. "And I'll bring Suzie, my new Featherweight."

Sarah laughed and said, "Of course. Caitlyn is going to be using mine. With three machines going, we'll have our part of this project done in no time." She pulled out a pad of paper and began drafting a simple design.

"Caitlyn is interested in the idea of charm quilts, so why don't we cut some of our fabric into five-inch squares and make the first placemats very simple," Sarah suggested. "If we place just three down and four across with a quarter-inch seam allowance, we'll make a placemat that is certainly close enough to the size they want."

"I like that idea. Let's keep it simple, especially since I'm new at this machine piecing." Sophie had been piecing by hand until she discovered the little antique Singer Featherweight in a consignment shop the previous year. "I've only used my machine to sew strips together for a simple table runner. I didn't show that to you yet."

"May I see it now?" Sarah asked.

"I'll go get it if you insist, but I'm really embarrassed to show it to you. It came out all cockeyed." Sophie left the room and returned with a table runner made using two-and-a-half-inch strips. "See? By the time I got to the last row, the whole thing had become all catawampus."

"We can fix this, Sophie, and the colors are beautiful." Sophie had bought the pre-cut strips on a roll from Ruth's shop and didn't realize how colorful it would be until she spread out the individual pieces.

"I like the colors," Sophie admitted. "Let's do the place-mats first, and then we can fix this."

Sarah finished her coffee and stood to leave. "Come on over around 12:00. I have soup in the Crock-Pot for the three of us, and we'll start working right after that."

"Charles isn't joining us?"

"I don't know if he'll be back," Sarah responded as she reached for her umbrella. "He's at the nursing home this morning nosing around. I reminded him of what he's always telling us—'Stay out of it'—but he said it's okay for him since he's a professional cop."

"Retired," Sophie clarified.

"Yes, retired. Let's hope he doesn't get involved. His doctors keep telling him to limit the stress, but you know him."

Sophie walked her to the door and offered to drive her home, but Sarah enjoyed walking in the rain. "It's just a drizzle," she said as she snapped the leash onto Barney's new harness. "See you later."

Chapter 5

"I see that Austin Bailey has canceled all his perfor-mances for the next few months," Charles said a few days later as he was reading the morning paper at the kitchen table.

"Really?" Sarah questioned. "Does it say why?"

"It doesn't say in the paper, but Hal told me Austin's going to stay in town until the young girl's murder is solved."

"Murder?" Sarah inquired, looking surprised. "When did it become a murder? I thought they said it was an accident." She tossed the dish towel across her shoulder and sat down at the table. "What's going on?"

"Hal got the medical examiner's report yesterday, and it was suspicious. He found traces of a rare substance in her system, which may have been the cause of death. They're investigating it as a possible homicide. It's unlikely she ingested it on purpose."

"Why didn't you tell me this yesterday?" Sarah asked with annoyance.

"Sorry, hon, but Hal didn't call me until after ten last night, and you were already in bed."

Sarah thought back to the previous evening and realized he was right. He had been watching a violent movie, and she knew she wouldn't sleep if she started watching it with him. She had taken a book and gone to bed early. "I fell asleep on the first page of my book," she said. "I'm glad you didn't wake me, but tell me what he said."

"That's about it. They don't have any suspects, and Madison was hired to talk to her family and friends in Missouri to rule out the possibility of suicide, although that doesn't seem likely."

"Who's Madison? I don't remember you mentioning the name before."

"Hank Madison. He just moved here from Hamilton. He worked undercover most of his career—just retired and wasn't ready to give it up completely. He's taking my place doing contract work for the department."

Taking your place? she wanted to ask but didn't. *Could it be he's going to cut back on police work?* Despite the strokes he had suffered, her husband had continued to stay involved in department cases at some level. He was already poking around in the Padilla case on his own.

"Did you learn anything the other day when you were talking to people at the nursing home? We never talked about that."

"One thing," Charles replied. "I found out why the girl was working in the nursing home. Austin Bailey had arranged it so she could help care for his grandmother. She was assigned exclusively to Mrs. Henderson, but they kept her on after his grandmother died to help with another woman for a few weeks. She was scheduled to go back to school soon."

"She was a nurse?" Sarah asked.

"No, she was there as a companion," he clarified.

"That's interesting. And she was the daughter of one of Austin's friends?"

"Yes, that's what I understand."

"Hmm," Sarah responded speculatively. "Did you learn anything else?"

"No, the nursing home staff is just scrambling to make sure they aren't liable for anything."

"Is it okay to share this new information with Sophie? The fact that the Padilla girl may have been murdered wasn't in the paper today, was it? I only glanced at the front page."

"No, but it's probably on television by now. You can see the network vans lined up in front of the nursing home from here."

"Do you have any idea where Austin is staying?" Sarah asked, and then thoughtfully added, "I guess they won't be able to keep his presence quiet any longer."

"No, but for now they have him safely stashed away. I think he should get out of town until this is solved. By the way, you've been asking a lot of questions, my dear wife. You and Sophie aren't up to anything, are you? You know what we agreed to …"

"Absolutely not, Charles." He noticed her eyebrows were a little high and her eyes a little wide.

"Sarah?"

Ignoring him, Sarah removed their Western omelet casserole from the oven.

The couple had breakfast, and Charles offered to clean the kitchen while she walked Barney. "I think I'll take some fabric and stop at Sophie's house for a few hours. We want to make a few more placemats before the meeting." Working together, she and Sophie had already made a dozen placemats, and Caitlyn had completed four. Sarah had designed another pattern using Sophie's leftover strips and some she had cut from her batik collection. They were both eager to try it out.

"In fact, I think I'll drive over and take my Featherweight."

"You're going to take Barney for a ride instead of a walk?" Charles said teasingly.

"Oh, that's right. Well, it only weighs eleven pounds. I'll put it in my canvas tote bag along with the fabric."

"I have a better idea," Charles said. "I'll walk along with you and carry the machine. You'll have your hands full with Barney and your supplies."

Sarah started to object. She wanted to get right to work and knew they'd lose much time once Charles and Sophie started talking about the case. But Charles seemed to read her mind, as he so often did. "And I won't even go inside. I'll leave you at the door and come right back. I want to get to the gym early this morning."

"Thank you," she responded as she gave him a quick peck on the cheek. "I'll go get my things together."

By the time she returned to the kitchen, their few dishes had vanished into the dishwasher, and the casserole dish had been washed and put away. Noticing that she was clearly pleased, he pulled her to him and kissed her warmly. "All this kitchen help deserves more than that little peck on the cheek you gave me earlier, don't you think?" he teased.

* * * * *

"Murder?" Sophie exclaimed. "The girl was murdered?"

"They don't know that for sure, but there was a drug in her body that was determined to be the cause of death. It doesn't mean someone poisoned her. She may have taken it herself, but they are investigating it as a murder."

"Someone should talk to her friends," Sophie suggested. "They would know if there was any chance she was suicidal. Perhaps we …"

"Stop, Sophie. They already have someone doing that." She told Sophie what Charles had told her about Hank Madison and his assignment. Then she began talking about how the presence of this man might mean Charles wouldn't be involved as deeply in cases as he had been when Matt was alive. "I worry about him, Sophie. Two major strokes and who knows how many small ones that no one detected. He just gets so intense when he's working on a case."

"It's up to us to take the pressure off of him," Sophie responded. "We can …"

"No, Sophie. We are staying out of this, remember? We promised Charles, and the police don't need our help anyway. Now, start sewing."

They spent the rest of the morning at their machines and finished four placemats each. "There are another eight," Sarah said. "With the ones we did last week and the ones Caitlyn made, we'll be going into that meeting with an impressive pile."

"I hope ours aren't too simple," Sophie said. "I know people like Delores will have made fancy ones."

"It won't matter. The people who receive them will love them. Just look at our colors! They're so cheerful."

"I wonder if anyone at the nursing home saw anything," Sophie said totally out of context. "Perhaps we …"

"Sophie!"

"Okay, okay," Sophie continued. "Do you want to drive over to Stitches and buy another roll of two-and-a-half-inch strips? We could split it and make several more tomorrow."

"I have Barney," Sarah began, looking at the two dogs curled up together on Emma's blanket.

"He can stay here with Emma. They're both sleeping, and we won't be gone long."

"Let's go," Sarah initiated, standing up eagerly. "I'll never turn down a fabric shopping trip."

* * * * *

"Sarah, I was getting ready to call you," Ruth announced as the two women entered the shop.

"Well, here I am," Sarah replied. Sarah privately hoped Ruth wasn't going to ask her to take on another teaching assignment. She was beginning to feel overwhelmed by her schedule and hoped to slow down and enjoy a bit of the remaining summer.

"It's Peggy. I'm worried."

"What happened?" Sarah asked.

"A woman brought in Peggy's placemats and said that Peggy wasn't going to be able to come to the quilt club anymore."

"Did she say why?"

"She was very vague, and she left before I could ask any questions. I was calling you earlier to ask you if you thought we should do anything."

"Such as?" Sarah asked. No one in the club knew Peggy very well. She attended sporadically and rarely spoke but seemed to be a skilled quilter. She seldom brought any of her projects to share with the group, but when she did they were exquisite.

"Oh, maybe call her or stop in to see her," Ruth responded. "I don't know. I just feel bad about it, and I appreciate the fact that she thought to get those placemats into the shop for us."

"Personally, I think we should leave her alone for now." Sarah decided not to mention the bruises she had seen. "Let's just see if she comes back on her own. She seems like a very private person to me," Sarah added.

Ruth began to say something but seemed to be having second thoughts.

"What?" Sarah asked. "Is there more?"

"Not really. I just have a bad feeling about this," Ruth declared. "She was in the shop last week and wore her sunglasses the whole time."

"Well, it is sunny just about every day," Sophie said.

"Yes, but who would be choosing fabric in the dark? I saw her slip them off for a moment to look more closely at the new line, but she put them right back on before I could see her face. I think she might have been hiding something."

"Like what? A black eye?" Sophie asked. "Maybe she had a fall."

"Maybe," Ruth responded tentatively. Just then there was a soft jingle announcing that someone had entered the shop. "I agree that she seems very private and might be offended by us descending on her right now," Ruth added as she stood to help her customer. "Let's hold off for now."

Sarah and Sophie picked out their strip sets, but their excitement had waned somewhat. They decided to buy one each since Ruth was having a 30% off sale on pre-cuts. Sophie bought another batik set in cool shades of blue, green, and gray, while Sarah chose a modern floral set in bright shades of red, yellow, and orange. They had both decided to make additional placemats as Christmas presents for their families. Sarah pulled a book off the shelf and showed Sophie the Rail Fence quilt pattern, and they both decided to use the design for their next few placemats.

They also found some bolts featuring large pieces of fruit. They realized they would be able to use this fabric as it was without piecing it. Sophie got a piece with apples, and Sarah found some pears. Each bought a yard and figured they could get at least four placemats out of each yard.

"What about backs?" Sophie asked suddenly as the fabric was being cut.

"We can use that red-and-white checked fabric I had left over from the kitchen curtains."

As they were leaving the quilt shop, they glanced across the street at the café. "Shall we?" Sarah asked.

"It's lunchtime," Sophie responded.

"That's a good enough reason," Sarah agreed, and they hurried across the busy street arm in arm.

Chapter 6

The quilters were crowded around the worktable sorting through the piles of pieced placemat tops and some placemats that were totally completed. The group had almost met their goal by the end of the previous meeting and tonight had been set aside for completing the placemats.

"Let's make two piles," Sophie suggested. "The ones that are ready to go and the ones that need batting and backs."

"There are three over here with the backs already attached but they aren't quilted," Delores said.

"Those are mine," Allison announced. "I wasn't sure how we were going to quilt them."

"Here are two more that only need quilting," someone called out.

"Okay," Sophie responded. "We'll make three piles, and then let's count them."

As the piles began to take shape, Sarah began counting. "Okay, we have sixty-two total. Twenty-eight are ready to go, and the rest need some work."

"I'll take the five that only need to be quilted," Delores announced. "If the rest of you will stitch those tops to their batting and backs, and get them turned and pressed, you can pass them to me, and I'll do all the quilting."

"I don't think we need everyone doing that," Ruth said. "How about if Anna and I start making more. I have some small panels that will work fine with just borders. We can whip those up very quickly."

Few words were spoken for the next couple of hours as machines buzzed.

"Finished!" Delores announced as she held up the last placemat. "Let's make a fresh pot of coffee and pull out the goodies." Ruth had brought croissants from the café across the street and Sophie had brought a pan of brownies. Everyone was moving into the kitchen to get refreshments, but Kimberly and her sister Christina remained behind, organizing the piles and doing a final count. "We have seventy-three, and I think we needed at least 103, didn't we?"

"Oh, wait," Ruth exclaimed. "I have more." She hurried to the front of the shop and pulled out a bag from under the counter, which contained ten more completed placemats.

"Where did those come from?" someone asked.

"Peggy's friend brought them in. She said Peggy couldn't make it tonight." Ruth had decided to leave out the rest of the story since it consisted primarily of speculation.

Moving on, Ruth announced, "Let's make plans for the last couple dozen placemats. Do you want to continue making them at home like we've been doing? If we do that, I think we can get them all finished at the next meeting."

The group agreed and pulled out the scrap baskets to choose more fabric to take home. No one mentioned Peggy again, but as they added the ten placemats Peggy had contributed, Sarah said, "These are really beautiful."

Peggy had used cheerful spring colors and taken the time to create interesting designs with half-square triangles. "She put lots of work into these," she added softly.

On their way home, Sarah confided in Sophie that she had seen bruises on Peggy and was beginning to wonder if perhaps she needed their help.

"Well, of course she does," Sophie exclaimed. "We'll go see her tomorrow."

"Not tomorrow, Sophie," Sarah responded. "But if she doesn't come to the next meeting, I think we should drop in on her and just make sure she's okay."

* * * * *

"What have you learned about the investigation?" Sarah asked her husband as they were preparing breakfast the next morning. Mornings had turned out to be the time that she and Charles were able to set the rest of the world aside and catch up on their lives. Both were very independent, having their own priorities and projects. Sarah liked it that way. She could never have been happy in a relationship where one partner's activities and happiness depended on the other person. But the sharing they did in the mornings had become a very special part of their relationship.

"I talked to Hal yesterday, and they have been questioning Austin. Hal called him a 'person of interest.'"

"What?" Sarah exclaimed, laying the pot holder down and turning to give Charles her full attention. "Why would they think Austin Bailey had anything to do with her death? He's a good friend of her father and has known Angela since she was a child."

"I know, and he's been helping her with her career. It doesn't make any sense, but you know they always look at family and people around the victim first."

"Well, I hope they start looking in more appropriate places. They need to find whoever did this to her. Imagine killing a talented young woman like Angela. It would have to be a very disturbed person. Have they talked to her friends?"

"I think so. Hal isn't as forthcoming with me as he used to be. I guess now that he has this Madison guy helping out, he's reluctant to share too much outside the department." He immediately realized how hard it was to say—to refer to himself as being outside the department.

"You don't suppose he's holding back because of Sophie and me, do you?" The two women had a history of interfering with police investigations when the victim was one of their friends or someone they cared about, which was just about everyone in the retirement community.

"I doubt it. I think he's just holding this one close to the vest because of the publicity that's been stirred up. Hal's been mentioned in the papers every day this week, and that's the last thing he wants to see."

"I've offered to poke around at the nursing home and have actually attempted that on my own but without any success."

"Wait. . . . What do you mean?" Sarah asked.

"Well, the administration has closed ranks. They're afraid the publicity is going to hurt business."

"Surely they can't be blamed just because someone was killed in their facility."

"You wouldn't think so," Charles responded. "But, you know, it's human nature. And the press isn't helping in that regard. Have you been reading the articles?"

Sarah nodded as she brought the platter of egg casserole and sausage to the table and pulled the toast out of the warming oven.

They didn't speak for the next few minutes as they enjoyed their meal. Sarah had added a variety of sautéed vegetables to the egg dish—thin slices of asparagus and onions, small broccoli flowerets, and finely diced summer squash. She had initially intended to include slices of sausage but decided to serve the links on the side since Charles especially enjoyed them. She didn't mention that they were turkey links rather than pork, and he didn't seem to notice.

"What do you and Sophie have planned today?" Charles asked as he drained the small glass of orange juice. "More placemats?"

"No," Sarah replied thoughtfully. "I'm scheduled to visit Sonya Lang today." She wondered whether she might be able to ask around while there. *Perhaps someone saw something*, she thought but definitely didn't say.

"So you'll be at the nursing home today?" he inquired, since she had sounded somewhat reticent about her plans.

"I guess so," she replied. "It's just …"

"What's bothering you, hon?" Charles asked.

"I just keep thinking about poor Angela. Someone wanted that young girl dead, and I just can't imagine why—or who, for that matter. How could a girl her age have an enemy that hated her enough to kill her?"

"People kill for many reasons, not just hate. He could be deranged, and she might have been the one he killed simply because she was there."

"You think that's possible?" Sarah asked doubtfully. "I wish we knew more about her. Do you know where she called home? Was she from Austin's hometown?"

"Yes, Austin said she lived with her parents in Missouri—Elkins, I think. It's Austin's hometown, too, and about four hours from here."

"That's Sophie's hometown, too, you know."

"I know," Charles responded. "Did she know any of these families?"

"Oh no. She left right after high school, over sixty years ago. I don't think she has any family left there." Suddenly Sarah perked up, realizing what Charles had just said. "Wait a minute! You were quoting what Austin said. You talked to Austin? When? Where?" Sarah became very excited as she fired questions at Charles.

"No, and calm down," Charles said, laughing. "I didn't speak with him directly. I meant to tell you about that."

"Okay, so tell me now. What did he say? When? And what does 'not directly' mean?"

"Just a minute," Charles exclaimed with a chuckle. "Just a minute. One question at a time."

"Just tell me everything," Sarah demanded. "From the beginning."

"Okay, I was at the department the day they brought him in for questioning. Hal asked if I'd like to sit in the viewing room next door."

"Did Hal say why he wanted you there?"

"No, but my guess is that he wanted my take on the guy. Anyway, during the interview, Bailey explained that he'd known the Padillas since high school. His friend Josh had married a girl in Austin's class, and Austin was best man at their wedding. Their daughter, Angela, was born a couple of years later, and Austin had been a part of their family functions until he started traveling with the band."

"What did he have to say about the daughter's death?"

"I'm getting to that, but first I want to tell you about his relationship with her. She called him Uncle Austin, and early on she showed a strong singing talent. He worked with her, sang with her, and in fact paid for her singing lessons. He said she had professional potential."

"And that's why she was going to be singing with him that afternoon?"

"Yes, but she didn't do that regularly. She was in college, and her father was insisting that she concentrate on her studies for now."

"So what else did they talk about?" Sarah asked, still curious about his close encounter with Austin Bailey.

"There were all those cop questions: 'Where were you at the time? Do you have any idea what happened? What did you see or hear?' All that sort of thing, but Austin didn't know a thing. He said he had just left his makeshift dressing room and was backstage preparing for the concert."

"So did you get a chance to speak with him personally?" Sarah asked.

"No, he left before Hal came to talk to me about my impressions."

"And your impressions?" she asked.

"There's no way this guy was involved in her murder if it even was a murder."

"Are the police still not sure?"

"Oh, they're saying murder, for sure, but who knows what goes on in the minds of these young folks."

"You're thinking suicide, Charles?"

"Well, maybe. I think everything should be considered."

"And the police aren't considering it? Didn't they send that new man Madison to talk to her friends?"

"Yeah, but he didn't get anything."

Someone needs to be talking with Angela's friends, Sarah said to herself. *And not a male ex-undercover cop. This is a job for grandmothers, and I think I know just the ones for the job.*

"I'm off to the gym," Charles announced, abruptly standing and heading for the garage door. He threw his wife a kiss and suggested, "Pizza tonight?"

"Sounds good," she agreed. While Sarah listened to the car backing out of the driveway, she dialed Sophie's phone number. When her friend answered, she asked, "Are you up for a road trip? There's detecting to be done."

As she was hanging up the phone, she heard a loud "Whoopee!" from the other end of the line.

Chapter 7

"How are we getting away with this?" Sophie asked as they pulled away from the curb, having loaded Sophie's overnight bag; a tote bag containing her infamous card file box; and her dog, Emma.

"I told Charles the absolute truth. We are taking the *Quilters' Travel Companion*, which directs us to every quilt shop within hundreds of miles of our house, and we'll be gone for two days, including one overnight stay."

"And he bought that?"

"Why wouldn't he? Those two facts are absolutely true. Here's the travel book right here, and we're actually stopping at a couple of the shops. And here's our motel reservation for tonight. Oh, and by the way, it's in Elkins, Missouri, but I didn't mention that, at least not at first."

"I'm surprised you were able to keep our true intentions from Charles," Sophie said. "He can usually see right through you."

"Well, the truth is it took him a while, but before the evening was over, he asked if we had an ulterior motive for this trip and I had to admit the truth."

"Was he upset?"

"Not so much. I convinced him that we wouldn't be in any danger just meeting a couple of young girls in a coffee shop. I had to promise him that if we learned anything, we'd come back to him with it and not follow up on it ourselves."

"That's reasonable," Sophie responded. "Now, let's get this dog over to Penny and get on the road."

Penny, born Penelope, was Sophie's granddaughter but she had only been in Sophie's life for the last couple of years. In fact, Sophie's son, Timothy, hadn't known about his daughter himself until Penny's mother, then dying of cancer, had contacted him when the girl was thirteen and asked him to take custody of her. The mother had chosen to raise the child alone and hadn't told Tim about her pregnancy. Tim took the girl, retired from his lifelong career with the Alaska pipeline, and returned to Middletown. Sophie became the grandmother of a teenager in her mid-seventies and couldn't have been happier.

"How does Emma get along with Blossom these days?" Sarah asked. "I know there was some jealousy going on there for a while." Blossom was Penny's papillon-Maltese mix and an adorable little dog.

"Those dogs are best friends now. Emma thinks she is Blossom's mother and the little one is eating up all the attention."

They dropped off the dog and ten minutes later were on the road heading toward Missouri.

"What's our plan?" Sophie asked after they'd been driving for a while.

"Well, first of all, we have an appointment at 4:00 to meet with Clarissa Wellington, Angela's best friend."

"How did you find out about her? Did Charles give you her name?"

"No, I called Josh Padilla, Angela's father, and told him what we were thinking about doing, and he was very cooperative. He gave me her best friend's name and number and invited us to their house tomorrow morning."

"You told him we were looking for any indication that she might have been suicidal?"

"No, Sophie. I couldn't bring myself to say that to a grieving father. Besides, I think it would have hurt our chances of meeting with them. I just told him we were looking for any clues as to what might have happened—any little piece of information her friends might have that could turn out to help in the investigation."

"That's actually the truth," Sophie responded thoughtfully.

"Grab the *Quilters' Travel Companion*," Sarah suddenly said, pointing to the tote bag between them. "I think this is our exit coming up."

"We're nowhere near Elkins yet," Sophie objected.

"Not for Elkins. For our first quilt shop." The two women excitedly reached 406 Main Street.

"This is it," Sarah announced as she pulled up the emergency brake and grabbed quarters out of the glove box for the parking meter. The two women stood in front of the store, admiring the stunning wedding quilt that was hanging in the window. The quilt featured interlocking bargello hearts in shades of blue, purple, and pale yellow. Posed next to the quilt was a graceful mannequin dressed in an antique wedding gown.

"What a beautiful display," Sophie said with a sigh as she attempted to take in all the details of the quilt.

An hour later they were back on the road with two bags each of fat quarters and a few yards of coordinated fabric. Most of their time had been spent listening to the shop owner as she shared the details of her daughter's wedding. "I'm glad you had a chance to see the quilt," the woman had said. "My daughter will be back from her honeymoon next weekend, and I'll have to pull it out of my window and give it back to her."

They had only driven a few minutes when Sophie asked, "Where's the next quilt shop?"

"Take a look at the book," Sarah replied. "I think there's one in the next town. I don't want to stop at all of them, but I spent money on this quilters' travel book, so we really *must* stop at a few to get my money's worth, don't you think?" Sarah announced with a devious smile.

"Of course, we must," Sophie responded, trying to sound like it was a terrible imposition when in fact it was quickly becoming one of her favorite pastimes.

They arrived in Elkins six hours after leaving home. The direct route would have taken much less time, but their second stop had been at an Amish quilt shop and restaurant where they swooned over both the quilts and the food. They both had ordered chicken and dumplings made with wide homemade noodles; big chunks of chicken; lots of vegetables; and a thick, creamy sauce. They vowed to stop there on their way home for pie.

"Should we go ahead and check into the motel?" Sophie asked. "I'd like to put my feet up for a few minutes."

"They said we could check in after 3:00, but in a small town like this I'm sure they won't be busy." As it turned out, they were right and had the opportunity to get settled in before meeting with Clarissa and a few of her friends. They planned to meet with Angela's father the next morning and hoped to leave for home by noon.

"Is there anything else you want to do while we're here?" Sarah asked, knowing that Sophie had lived in Elkins when she was young. "You went to high school here, didn't you?"

"That was sixty-five years ago, Sarah. Nothing will be the same. I don't think I want to see what's become of it. I like my memories. Let's just get our interviews done."

* * * * *

Sarah was surprised when she entered the café and saw the young women. She knew they were Angela's friends from high school, and in her mind she had been picturing them much younger. In fact, there were four well-dressed professional-looking women sitting around the table, obviously waiting for them. One of the women stood and extended her hand, introducing herself as Clarissa Wellington. "These are Angie's other close friends, Kate, Megan, and Samantha." The women squeezed in closer to make room for Sarah and Sophie. The tables were somewhat small, but there was only one other customer in the café at the time.

"Let's pull that other table over," Samantha suggested, and within moments they were comfortably spread out and the waitress was taking their orders for coffee and tea.

"What do you have that's good?" Sophie asked, straining to see what was in the pastry display.

"Let me bring out a tray," the woman replied as she headed for the counter. Moments later she returned with an assortment of delectable-looking pastries.

"I'll take this one and that one over there," Sophie said as she surveyed the choices.

Two of the young women—the slender ones, Sarah noted—chose to have coffee only, and the other two ordered biscotti. Sarah chose a pastry covered with almonds.

"Good choice," the waitress said with a pleasant smile.

"I want to thank you all for taking the time to meet with us," Sarah began. "I know you must be busy. You're in real estate, Clarissa?"

"Yes, Kate and I work together. Megan just started working at the bank, and Samantha, as you can clearly see," she teased, "is starting a family."

Samantha blushed and gently touched her swollen abdomen. "Three more months," she said proudly.

"Well," Sarah responded, "I'm sure you all need to get back to your lives, and we appreciate you taking the time to talk with us."

"If it can help catch the person who did this to our friend, we're happy to do it," Kate replied. "I'm not sure how we can help, though."

"I know you've already talked with an investigator from the police department, but Sophie and I thought you just might have thought of something that could help the police find the person who took Angela's life."

"We've talked about it," Clarissa went on, "but since it happened so far away we don't know how we can help. We all would get texts from Angie now and then, but she didn't say much."

"I told that detective all I knew," Samantha commented. "Well," she added, "except I forgot about Nathan."

"Nathan?" Sophie questioned.

"A guy she went out with here in town before she went to Middletown. I think he went to see her in Middletown a time or two."

"Did anyone tell the detective about him?" Sarah asked.

"I started to," Kate spoke up, "but I didn't know his last name, and it was a long time ago. She stopped seeing him after a couple of dates."

Sophie had been making notes on her file cards as the women talked. "Does anyone know his last name?" she asked. They all shook their heads no.

"She wasn't all that into the guy," Clarissa explained. "Actually," she added, looking at Samantha curiously, "I didn't even know he went up there to see her."

"Yeah, it was about a month ago."

"That might be important," Sarah suggested. "How can we get his last name?"

"I know a girl he used to date." Kate pulled out her phone and with a couple clicks had the girl on the phone. Kate stood and moved away from the table to talk with her. She was gone for a surprisingly long time, and Sarah found herself glancing over every few minutes and watching the young woman's expression. *She looks worried*, Sarah thought.

The others engaged in a few minutes of light conversation until Kate returned. "His name is Caldwell. Nathan Caldwell," she announced very matter-of-factly and began to sip her tea. Sarah waited, hoping she would offer more information about the conversation, but none seemed to be forthcoming.

"Did she have anything to say about him?" Sarah finally asked.

Kate was hesitant. "Well, yes, but she asked me not to tell anyone."

"Do you think it might help Angela's family? They really need to know what happened to their daughter," Sarah affirmed.

"We all do," Samantha added, looking at her friend. "What did she say?"

With a deep sigh, Kate explained that the girl had dated him in high school but had broken up with him because he was very controlling. "He was always telling her what to do, what to wear—that sort of thing." Kate went on to say that after she broke up with him, he started stalking her. Everywhere she went he was there. At first she thought it was just coincidence, but finally she talked to her father about it, and he called the police.

"How did he take that?" Sarah asked.

"He was furious. Mary Ellen said she had to stop dating anyone because she was afraid of what he would do."

"How did it get resolved?"

"After a while, he just stopped."

"He probably got interested in someone else," Clarissa suggested.

"And you said he was interested in Angela," Sarah said thoughtfully, "and that she wasn't that into him, and he visited her in Middletown. I wonder if the same thing could have been going on."

The group sat around the table quietly for a few moments. All had solemn looks on their faces when the waitress stopped by looking worried. "Is everything okay?" she asked with concern. "Can I bring you anything?"

Sarah assured her everything was fine but asked for refills. "Anyone want more pastry?" she asked.

"Another cruller," Sophie chimed in. "But pick one without much icing. I'm on a very strict diet, you know." The group tried not to react, but Megan couldn't hold back a chuckle.

After their refills had been delivered, Clarissa looked at Sarah and asked, "What are you going to do with this information? Are you going to talk to him?"

"I don't think so," she responded, remembering her promise to her husband. "I think this is something for the official investigators, but I'll let them know. I'm sorry about not being able to keep your friend's secret, but I think this is more important. I think this Nathan Caldwell could be a person of interest to them."

For the next half hour, the young women shared stories about their friend Angie. They talked about her incredible voice and how fortunate it had been that she had Austin Bailey in her life. "He was opening doors for her. She would have become very famous," one of the young women noted.

"That's assuming she didn't blow it," Samantha grumbled.

"Don't go there," Clarissa advised.

"Why not?" Samantha protested. "They're looking for the whole story."

The table became silent. Only Sophie appeared to be ready to ask the question, but Sarah unobtrusively encouraged her to wait. She wanted to see who might speak up and share whatever they were holding back.

Finally, Clarissa sighed and said, "Okay, we'd been worried about her because she was getting a little wild the last year of school. I think that's why her father let her go to Middletown when Austin suggested it. He wanted to get her away from that crowd she was hanging with."

"I agree," Samantha said, "but it didn't help much. She was always texting about this roadie she was getting interested in, and he sure didn't sound like he was the kind of guy her father would have liked."

"Oh, come on, Samantha," Clarissa exclaimed. "She was just looking for some fun."

"Dangerous fun, if you ask me," Samantha muttered.

Changing the subject, Clarissa looked at Sarah and asked, "Do you know anything about the nursing home where she was working? Could they have been involved?"

"It's an excellent facility, and I'm sure that's why Austin chose it for his grandmother. I volunteer there and have nothing but good things to say about it. They're working closely with the police."

Sarah started to ask a question but appeared hesitant. Clarissa noticed and said, "Go on, Mrs. Parker. Is there something you want to ask?"

"Well, it's just that since poison was involved, there's been some question about whether your friend might have taken it on purpose. And we were just wondering …"

"Suicide? You were wondering if she might have killed herself?" Clarissa asked incredulously.

"Absolutely not!" Kate cried before Sarah could respond.

"We were just wondering …"

"Well, stop wondering. Angela was a happy, fun-loving young woman with a fantastic future that she was very excited about. Angela loved life more than anyone I ever knew," Kate declared.

"Whoever is thinking that is way off base," Clarissa concurred.

"I agree," Megan added.

"I'm sorry. I just had to ask," Sarah said apologetically.

"We understand," Clarissa replied, "but that's something that Angela would never do."

As they stood up to leave, Sarah thanked everyone for their willingness to meet and for their openness. Clarissa hugged them both, and as Sophie began collecting her file cards, Megan asked, "What do you do with those cards?"

"It's something I learned from a very famous detective. Well, not a real detective," Sophie clarified. "She's actually fictional and lives in a renovated garage in California, but this is the way she solves her cases. She puts all the facts on cards and shuffles them around until the answer pops out."

"And does that work for you?" Clarissa asked.

"Not yet," she responded as she looked down at her cards with a disgruntled frown. "But I keep hoping!"

* * * * *

"Sophie, I'm sorry to wake you up, but …"

"What? What's happening? Where am I?" Sophie asked, sounding both startled and confused.

"I'm sorry, Sophie. I didn't mean to startle you, but I wanted you to see something."

"Where?" she glanced up, looking around the room and seeing the clock. "It's only 2:00 in the morning. What do you want me to see?"

"It's outside. Put on your robe so we can step outside for a minute."

Sophie complied but was mumbling to herself as she slipped into her robe. Sarah opened the French doors to the balcony, and for the first time Sophie realized they were on the back side of the motel. They were looking out on an enclosed garden washed in moonlight and sparkling with dew-covered vines. There was a fountain in the center feeding a small pond. "Is that a big fish?" Sophie exclaimed.

"It is, but what I wanted you to see is the sky. I've never seen anything so spectacular."

Sophie looked up and caught her breath with a sudden gasp. There she stood under what looked like millions of stars glistening against the night sky.

"It looks like we could touch some of them from here," Sophie murmured, "yet others seem eternities away." The two women, arm in arm, strolled through the garden toward a stone bench without taking their eyes off the sky. "I don't think I've ever seen such a magnificent night sky," she added in a voice still barely above a whisper, not wanting to interrupt the tranquility of the moment.

"Do you forgive me for waking you up?" Sarah asked.

"I wouldn't have missed this for the world. It's magical," Sophie responded.

The two women didn't return to their room for another hour as they quietly basked in the beauty of the starlight.

Chapter 8

Despite their lack of sleep, they both woke up refreshed the next morning, and this time it was Sarah who momentarily didn't know where she was. It all became clear when she looked over and saw Sophie sitting by the window in her pink elephant pajamas, working on another hexagon project.

"What will this one be?" Sarah asked as she stretched and yawned.

"A quilt or a placemat, depending on when I get tired of making the hexagons," her friend replied. "I'm starving," she added. "Get dressed and let's get some breakfast."

Sarah looked at the clock and realized she'd slept later than she'd intended. "You're right," she agreed. "We're due at the Padillas' house at 10:00. I'd better get moving."

Later that morning, as they drove into the Padillas' neighborhood, Sophie observed that the community looked like something out of an old *Leave It to Beaver* episode. "Just look at those big old maples, and the houses all look so well kept."

As they pulled up in front of the Padilla house, Sarah noticed that the home appeared warm and inviting, with no indication of the unhappiness within. She had dreaded imposing on the dead girl's parents, but as they approached the house, Mr. Padilla opened the front door and welcomed them warmly.

Once they were seated in the spacious sitting room, Sarah said, "I want to thank you for giving me Clarissa's name, Mr. Padilla."

"Please call me Josh," the girl's father said in a gentle tone.

"And call me Sarah. Clarissa is a lovely young woman, and she brought three of Angela's friends along, as you suggested—Kate, Megan, and Samantha."

"I know them all, and they are fine young women. My daughter was a good judge of character and chose her friends well." He glanced at her picture on the mantel and dropped his eyes to hide the pain.

They spent the next half hour learning about Angela from her father's point of view, which, as it turned out, was very much as her friends had seen her—kind, helpful, happy, and excited about her future. He didn't mention the concerns Samantha, in particular, had brought up the day before.

"I'd like to ask you about a male friend of hers, a Nathan Caldwell," Sarah ventured. "Did you know him?"

"I never met the man, but I know that he wasn't a friend of hers. I think she went out with him a time or two, but she broke it off. She never mentioned why, but I'm sure she had a good reason. That was some time ago. Not relevant now."

"Did your daughter ever talk to you about the men she dated?" Sarah queried.

Mr. Padilla looked a bit regretful. "No, when she was still living at home she'd talk to her mother about those kinds of things. She never wanted me to have too many details." He let out a puff of air and almost smiled as he added, "She said

I embarrassed her with all my interrogation of the boys that came to pick her up."

Sarah smiled, remembering how her late husband had done the same thing whenever their daughter brought a boy home. For a moment she felt a pang of grief herself. *We never get over the loss of loved ones*, she thought. *We just learn to go on.*

Mrs. Padilla entered the room then, and her eyes were red and swollen. Sarah realized that this meeting was causing her additional pain. After the introductions, Mrs. Padilla, who apparently had been listening to their previous conversation, volunteered, "Angie told me about that Caldwell boy. She found him to be annoying and broke it off after a couple of dates. She never heard from him again."

Sophie, noticing the inconsistency with what the girl's friends had said, raised her eyebrows and looked at Sarah, but Sarah said nothing. Sarah had realized that Angela obviously hadn't discussed her concerns about Caldwell with her parents. *Was Angela afraid of this Nathan Caldwell?* Sarah wondered. *And why did he go to Middletown?*

"One other thing I'd like to ask, if you don't mind," Sarah began, glancing at Sophie, who nodded encouragement for her to continue. In the car that morning they had discussed asking Mr. Padilla about Angela's relationship with Austin.

Sarah posed the question, and Josh responded after first glancing at his wife. "You probably know that Austin's folks were killed and he grew up with his grandmother. She was an excellent parent, but I think Austin missed having a family atmosphere. He seemed to love all the hubbub that went on at our house with my brothers and me. It was always chaos," he said with a chuckle.

"So he spent a great deal of time at your house?" Sarah resumed.

"He sure did. His grandmother was always concerned that he was bothering my mother, but Mom loved him like one of her own. Anyway, when we went off to college, and I fell in love with Adelaide, the three of us were always together. He was my best man and was right there through two miscarriages and finally the miracle of Angela's birth. He was there for every birthday party, every school play, and spent a part of every holiday with us."

"So he is essentially a part of your family?"

"He's like a brother to me."

"And Angela?"

"She called him Uncle Austin and loved him right along with her other uncles. Maybe more," he added. "Did you know he taught her how to play the guitar? He also paid for more singing classes than I can count. She has—*had*—a spectacular voice. Austin was sure she'd make it big when the time came. I insisted that she finish school, but …" He looked away, unable to finish. "I'm sorry," he added.

"I appreciate your sharing this with us, Mr. Padilla." After a few moments, Sarah added, "I have one other question if you don't mind."

Mr. Padilla silently nodded permission for her to continue.

"Did either of you have any concerns about Angela's lifestyle or her friends?"

Mr. Padilla hesitated, then gently shook his head. "No, not really. Nothing that matters anymore."

They sat quietly for a few moments. Sarah was hoping that he would continue but didn't want to push since the Padillas were both under so much stress.

Mrs. Padilla, looking uncomfortable, broke the silence by offering them coffee. Sarah declined, saying that they needed to get back home, but as she stood to leave, the woman added, "If you can take a few minutes, I'd love to show you Angie's garden."

"We'd love to see it," Sarah replied, realizing this grieving mother needed to share a part of her memories with them. They followed Mrs. Padilla out the side door and found themselves inside a walled garden that immediately brought to mind the young Mary Lennox and her secret garden, from one of Sarah's favorite books from childhood.

"Angela would sit out here for hours reading," Mrs. Padilla said with a faraway look. "When she was very young, she'd play out here with her dolls, serving them tea and talking to them like friends. Later her friend Clarissa would come over, and they'd spend time with their heads together giggling, probably talking about boys," she added with a sad smile. Sarah was glad they had taken the time to come outside with the grief-stricken mother. It seemed to help her.

"I feel close to her here even though she didn't come into her garden much during the last few years," Mrs. Padilla added. "Josh won't even come out the door, much less sit out here with me." She led her visitors to an area where two benches faced each other and surrounding pots overflowed with flowering vines. They sat quietly for a while, and slowly Mrs. Padilla began to talk about her memories of her daughter, mostly as a young child.

Parents aren't meant to outlive their children, Sarah told herself as she sat with the heartbroken woman.

* * * * *

"Have you spoken to Charles today?" Sophie asked. They were back on the road and had decided not to stop at any quilt shops, as they were both eager to get home.

"I called him last night to let him know about our meeting with the girls."

"Is it okay now to call young women 'girls'?" Sophie asked. "I know that was out for a while."

"It's probably still frowned upon, but the older I get, the younger everyone else seems to be getting. I remember when we used to go visit my grandmother. I thought she was ancient," Sarah continued, "but I figured out the other day that she was probably only forty, nearly half my current age!"

"And you talk about age? Do you realize I'm almost eighty?"

"Eighty?" Sarah questioned with a frown. "Didn't we celebrate your seventy-fifth birthday last year?"

"That's right. And it's a year later."

"And what does that have to do with eighty?" Sarah asked, her forehead crinkled with lines of confusion.

"It's right around the corner now," Sophie announced. "And eighty is *old*."

"Eighty is just another number, Sophie, and I still need to insist that it's off in the future. You aren't eighty or anywhere near eighty." Before Sophie could respond, Sarah added, "And besides that, what difference would it make if you were turning eighty? It's just a number. In fact, eighty is actually the new sixty, and just look at you. You're taking on new hobbies and talking about taking computer classes. You travel, and let's not forget for a minute that you have a new boyfriend!"

"Humph."

"Well, it's true. You don't talk about him much, but Charles and I can't miss how often his car is sitting in front of your house."

"We're just friends," Sophie objected, looking out the window and away from Sarah.

"Is there a problem?" Sarah asked, wondering where the initial excitement had gone. Sophie had met Norman the previous year. A retired conference and wedding planner, he was still actively involved with his company despite his retirement, and he was obviously falling for Sophie.

"He's too young for me," Sophie muttered.

"Too young? He was just right for you last year. What happened?"

"Eighty happened. At least it's going to happen before we know it. Why would he want to be with an old woman?"

"Sophie, you're the same person you were last year, and he was obviously smitten then. He's crazy about you, and it wouldn't surprise me if he's thinking about marriage."

"Marriage?" Sophie screeched. "There's no way I would consider marriage at my age."

"I wasn't that much younger when I married Charles," Sarah pointed out.

"Yes, you were. You were in your early seventies. That's not eighty."

"And you're not eighty either!" Sarah exclaimed, becoming a bit impatient with her friend.

They had just pulled into a rest stop. Sophie sat quietly as Sarah opened her door and stepped out of the car. Since her friend hadn't moved, Sarah leaned back in and said, "Sophie? Are you coming? This is the last stop for another sixty miles."

Sophie sat looking somewhat dejected and didn't respond. "Sophie?"

Sophie sighed and began to stir. "Maybe I just need to get on the other side of eighty and see how I feel, assuming I'm still alive then."

Well, that's a clue, Sarah thought. "It sounds like you think eighty is the end of the road, Sophie. Just think about the people we take classes with at the center. Alice is in her nineties and just look at her. Did you know she won a medal in the swimming competition?"

"Perhaps I'm overreacting," Sophie conceded as she pulled herself out of the car with a grunt. "Maybe if I got my hip fixed …"

"Perhaps," Sarah responded, choosing not to repeat her advice on the hip replacement. *She'll do it when she's ready*, Sarah thought.

What Sophie had chosen not to share with her friend was the fact that Norman had, in fact, brought up the idea of marriage, and she had adamantly refused, saying that she had no interest in marriage. He had appeared to be hurt and had chosen to leave shortly afterward, when it had become clear that she would not discuss her feelings with him. The only time she had spoken to him since was to let him know about her upcoming trip to Missouri with Sarah. He had wished her well but had seemed remote.

By the time they got back on the road, the subject of age had been dropped. They talked about making a few more placemats so they'd have them on hand when they were needed again.

They'd been on the road about an hour when Sophie squealed, "Look up ahead!"

"What?!" Sarah reacted, swerving out of her lane and struggling to get the car back under control. "You scared me to death, Sophie."

"Sorry. It's that sign way up there. See it? *Herbie's Fabric Super Mart—discounted fabric—open daily.*"

"Okay, I got a glimpse of it. Where is it?"

"All I could see was *Exit 13*. We just crossed the Illinois state line, so it must be less than thirteen miles from here. Can we stop?" Sophie pleaded.

"Well, I guess we could," Sarah expressed hesitantly, "but I thought you were in a hurry to get home."

"Not if we miss seeing a fabric supermarket. Aren't you curious?"

"Well, actually I am," Sarah confessed with a sly grin. "Watch for the exit. Did the sign say where to go once we get off the highway?"

"You were swerving all over the road at that point. I didn't get a chance to read the rest of the sign."

I swerved because you were squealing, Sarah thought but decided not to say. At least her friend was now excited about the fabric store and not obsessing about her age. She noticed Sophie was now digging around in her gigantic purse and had pulled out her umbrella, a magazine, an apple, and a wad of fabric.

"What are you searching for?"

"My cell phone," Sophie responded. "I'll call and ask directions."

"Good idea," Sarah said with a nod. "Get their address too, so we can put it in the GPS so we don't get lost."

Sophie was still on the phone with the fabric store when Sarah pulled off at the exit. "Where to from here?" she asked impatiently.

"Oh," Sophie expressed with surprise. "I was supposed to ask you for directions from Exit 13." She had been asking the woman on the other end of the line about the store's fabric and how she got started in the business, and when Sarah interrupted with her question, Sophie was asking about the woman's grandchildren.

"Just give me the address, and I'll put it in the GPS," Sarah repeated.

Sarah pulled over into a wide graveled area and reached for the GPS. She began entering the address as Sophie repeated it. "What town are we in?" Sarah asked, and Sophie repeated the question to the woman on the other end of the line.

"We're only five minutes away," she said turning to Sarah. "You won't need that."

After Sophie hung up, Sarah began driving even though the address wasn't complete in the GPS.

"You just drive up this road to where the old Esso filling station used to be and turn left."

Sarah looked dumbfounded. "How will we know where it used to be?"

"Gracie said we'll see the hollowed-out remains."

"Gracie?"

"Yes, she's in charge of the emporium today."

"The emporium?"

"That's what Gracie calls it. That was its old name before Herbie took over."

"Herbie?" Sarah queried, but was immediately sorry, so she added, "Never mind about Herbie. Just tell me when to turn."

They drove several miles without seeing the remains of an old gas station. Finally, Sarah pulled over again and picked up Sophie's cell phone, which was now on the floor of the car. She looked under dialed calls and pressed Sophie's most recent call. "Hello," she said when the call was answered, presumably by Sophie's new friend, Gracie.

"Could you please tell me how to get to your store? We took Exit 13 and are driving east on …"

"Oh, honey, you're going the wrong way. Head back toward the highway, cross over it, drive about a mile and take a right-hand turn on Hixon Lane. We're on the right in about a mile. You can't miss us. 225 Hixon Lane."

"Thank you," Sarah responded with a relieved sigh. "We'll see you soon."

"Humph," Sophie snorted.

"What was that for?"

"Well, you talked to Gracie, and you don't know a thing about her. You have to ask questions. …"

"I asked my question, which was 'How do we get there?' "

"But what about all the other questions?" For the ten minutes that it took to drive to Herbie's Fabric Super Mart, Sophie filled Sarah in on the history of the store, the tragedy of how Herbie lost it, and the name of one of Gracie's grandchildren. "I didn't find out about her other grandchildren because you interrupted me."

"I'm sure you'll know all about them by the time we leave the store."

As they pulled into the parking lot, Sarah turned to Sophie and asked, "Since Herbie tragically lost the store, why is it still called 'Herbie's'?"

"Well," Sophie huffed as she turned to get out of the car. "You'll just have to find that out for yourself."

* * * * *

Both women gasped as they stepped into the building.

They found themselves in what appeared to be a large warehouse. From floor to ceiling and in all spots in between there was fabric. High shelves were stacked with multi-colored bolts. There were narrow aisles between rows and rows of fabric—some on bolts, some folded and packaged, some hanging out of bins.

"Would you like a basket, ladies?" A voice asked from behind a wall of fabric. The voice stepped out, pushing the largest grocery cart Sarah had ever seen.

"You must be Gracie," Sophie squealed, and the woman acknowledged with a nod that she was Gracie.

"And you must be the nice lady I spoke with," Gracie inferred with a welcoming smile. "Shall I show you around?"

"That might be a good idea," Sarah responded. "Right now I'm overwhelmed."

The three women were ambling down the crowded center aisle. "Okay," Gracie said, pointing toward the back of the store. "Back there on the right are the upholstery fabrics. Then we have linens and broadcloth in front of that, the silks start over there, and … oh, wait a minute. Are you girls quilters?"

"Yes," Sarah affirmed, but before she could say more, Gracie made a sweeping gesture to the left side of the store.

"Then you're in luck," she announced. "All the rest of the store is 100% cotton. We cater to quilters, as you can see." She then pointed out various designers, but added, "You'll have to dig through it all since things get mixed up in here."

"Look at these kittens," Sophie exclaimed, stopping at a colorful section that appeared to feature children's fabrics. "Penny loves kittens. What could I make for her?"

"Do you want to make another quilt?" Sarah asked tentatively, knowing that Sophie was already working on several projects.

They began pawing through the fabric, finding fabrics with toys; ducks; puppies; and children playing ball, riding bikes, and waving from their school bus. "Children would love anything made from these fabrics," Sarah commented.

"I was thinking of something small like … say! How about placemats? I've gotten really good at it, and I could whip up several for her." Sophie loved having a granddaughter to fuss over for the first time.

"That would be great," Sarah responded. "And look at these with little farm animals. I think Jonathan would love them." Sarah's grandson had just turned three. Jason and his wife, Jennifer, also had a six-year-old girl, Alaina, who Sarah was sure would love the kitten fabric as well.

After poking through the entire store, the two friends found that they had circled back to the children's fabrics. "This is so far from home, Sophie. I think we should load up on this fabric. We both have grandchildren, and the club frequently makes charity quilts for children. We can always use it …"

"And the price is right," Sophie added. "I agree."

The two women began filling the grocery cart until it was brimming with fun, playful fabrics. "These would make any child smile," Sophie said as they headed for a cutting table.

When they left Herbie's Fabric Super Mart, they had so many bags that Gracie had to come out with them to help them load the car. "You girls come back now, hear?" she called out as they were driving away.

"Why is the sun so low in the sky?" Sophie asked suddenly.

"It's late afternoon," Sarah responded.

"We missed lunch," Sophie exclaimed.

"If we stop, we'll get home pretty late."

"Well, we need to stop twice," Sophie pointed out. "Lunch and dinner."

"I think we can get by with one stop, Sophie, but I agree we need to stop, and I need to call Charles. He's probably already worrying since he was expecting us home by now."

"Look," Sophie squealed, again causing her driver to swerve. "A fried chicken place at the next exit."

"Okay, I'm game. Comfort food it is," Sarah agreed, and she pulled off the highway again, noticing that this was only Exit 16. "We're three miles closer to home than we were this morning," she said with a chuckle.

It was dark, and Sophie was dozing as they approached the Middletown city limits.

Chapter 9

"What did Hal have to say when you told him about Nathan Caldwell?" Sarah asked as she and Charles sat together enjoying their morning breakfast routine. She had eagerly told him all about her visit with Angela's friends and what they had said about Nathan and his obsession with the girl he had dated before Angela.

"First of all, he said he was very pleased that you didn't contact the Caldwell guy while you were in Elkins. The investigating officer wants to catch him completely off guard. I hope none of the girls you talked to will clue him in."

"That's very unlikely. They seemed to realize that the man could be dangerous, even if he isn't the person that killed their friend. And none of them knew him personally."

"Good. They're sending the new guy, Hank Madison, to Elkins tomorrow. They've already made contact with the department there and had Caldwell's record forwarded to them. They had much more on him than what you learned from Angela's friends. The guy's a loose cannon."

"Did you discuss what the girls said about Angela's zest for life? They said there was no chance their friend would have committed suicide."

"Yeah, I passed that on to him, but he didn't have much to say about it. The department never seriously considered the idea of suicide anyway. They're looking for the perp and, unfortunately, they've zeroed in on Austin."

"What possible motive do they think he had?"

"They're having trouble with that one. But the body was discovered in Austin's dressing room, where he had been shortly before that. He knew Angela, and because they were such close friends, some of the guys in the band speculated that they might have been having an affair."

"Oh, nonsense," Sarah replied. "Everything we've heard sounds like he considered Angela as family. He'd known her since she was a baby."

"But that's exactly where investigators look first—family, friends, coworkers. Most murders are committed by someone known to the victim. Very few are actually killed by strangers."

"That's exactly why they need to be looking at this Caldwell guy," Sarah exclaimed.

"They will, dear. They will," Charles said, rubbing her back reassuringly. "What do you say we head up the road in a couple of hours and have lunch at that new Thai place on the pike?"

"Good idea," Sarah responded, knowing that was just the distraction she needed to put the murder aside. "And that can be our main meal of the day," she added, "since I have quilt club tonight."

At that moment the phone rang, and Charles heard his wife explaining to the caller that they wouldn't be presenting the placemats to the Meals on Wheels folks until the next meeting. "Sure," he heard her say. "It would be fine to miss the meeting, Sophie. What's going on?" After a long silence on Sarah's end, she finally said, "I'm glad to hear you say that, Sophie. You two have a wonderful evening."

"What's going on?" he asked when she hung up.

"Sophie can't make the meeting tonight," was all his wife offered by way of explanation. He was curious but decided not to press.

* * * * *

"So how was your date last night?" Sarah asked when Sophie arrived for their quilting appointment the next day.

Sophie waved her friend's question away, saying, "Later. First, look what I brought." She pulled out her Featherweight machine, a huge bag of five-inch squares, and a book entitled *Nickel Quilts for Beginners*.

"And all of these are different?" Sarah asked, picking up the bag of pre-cut squares.

"That's what it said on the website. I haven't opened it yet, but it said they were all different. Two hundred and fifty of them."

"Is that enough to make a quilt?" Sarah asked, making some quick calculations in her head.

"I'd probably need that much again if I made a quilt, but actually I'm thinking about making a tablecloth."

"Oh, that would look wonderful in your kitchen," Sarah suggested enthusiastically, picturing Sophie's antiques and country decor.

Sophie spread her things out on the folding table Charles had set up for her. "May I ask my question now?" Sarah queried.

"Go ahead," Sophie responded with a sigh.

"How was your date last night?"

At first Sophie was quiet, but a slow smile began to spread across her face. "It was wonderful," she answered with the suggestion of a flush appearing on her cheeks.

Sarah wanted to grab her friend up in a big bear hug but held back, knowing Sophie wouldn't like that. Instead, she just clapped her hands with joy and said, "So you and Norman have worked things out."

"Yes, I would say so," Sophie acknowledged, trying to control her smile.

Sophie's body language made it clear she didn't want to discuss her evening with Norman in any detail. They'd been at odds since their last trip to his cabin in Kentucky, but Sophie had never wanted to share the details. *At least it's resolved*, Sarah thought but didn't say.

Sophie began tearing open her bag of fabric and spread the small pieces out. "Just look," she announced, sounding pleased. "They're exactly what I was picturing for my kitchen. This is definitely going to be a tablecloth. Pass me your calculator so I can figure out if I have enough." She pulled a notebook out of her tote bag, and Sarah could hear her mumbling some numbers, but then in a louder voice she said, "Sarah, I need your help. How many of these five-inch squares will I need?"

At that moment Charles appeared in the doorway. "What's going on in here?" he asked.

"You're just the person we need," Sarah declared. She was perfectly capable of calculating the fabric requirements for Sophie's table quilt, but she wanted him to feel included, so she told him the dimensions of the table, the size of the finished blocks, and the preferred drop. "How many squares will she need?"

Charles looked a bit confused, but once Sophie handed him her pad with the dimensions she wanted, he made a few quick calculations and replied, "Well, 266 pieces will make it a little short and 280 will make it a little long."

"I'll go with it being a little long, and I'll need thirty more squares," Sophie decided. "I already have 250."

"We can probably cut the thirty out of our stash," Sarah suggested.

"By the way," Sophie said to Sarah as Charles was leaving the room. "Was Peggy at the meeting last night?"

"No, and I didn't think she would be. Remember, her friend said she wasn't coming back."

"Do you think it's time to stop in and check on her?"

"Don't do it today," Charles hollered from the hallway before Sarah could respond.

"Why not?" Sarah hollered back.

Charles returned to the sewing room with a mischievous look on his face. "Because we're having company this afternoon."

"I should leave," Sophie responded, beginning to pick up her fabric.

"No," Charles replied. "Our guest especially wants to see you."

"Me?" Sophie said, looking surprised.

"Who is this mysterious guest?" Sarah asked.

"You'll see," Charles teased as he started back down the hall toward his den.

"Wait," Sarah cried, hurrying after him. "I need to know who's coming. We will need refreshments …"

"Taken care of," Charles replied. "Just go back to your sewing. Everything is under control."

"What in the world do you think he's up to?" Sophie asked when Sarah returned.

"I don't know, but he's adamant that we stay out of it, so let's just stick with what we're doing."

An hour later the doorbell rang. Sarah and Sophie both headed for the living room, but Charles got there first. "There you go. Keep the change," he was saying. The women smelled pizza.

"You think that's the mysterious surprise? He bought us pizza?"

"My guess is that we're serving pizza to the mysterious guest."

"Go back to your sewing," Charles said as he headed for the kitchen. Sarah followed him and saw him put the two pizzas in the warming oven.

"What's going on?" she asked, beginning to feel a bit irritated with her husband.

At that moment the doorbell rang again, and Charles called out to Sophie, "Sophie, would you get the door?"

"Why Sophie? It's our door," Sarah grumbled, unable to hide her irritation.

"You'll see," he responded with a twinkle in his eye, which added to her annoyance.

A moment later they heard a screech coming from the front of the house. Sarah hurried to the entryway to see what was going on, only to find her friend Sophie with her arms around the waist of a very tall and handsome young man wearing cowboy boots and a fancy braided bolo tie.

"Good grief," Sarah cried. "It's Austin Bailey!"

Chapter 10

"So there I was talking to the nursing home adminis-trator," Charles was saying as he sat holding a beer in one hand and a drooping piece of pizza in the other, "when who should come sauntering into the office but this cowboy here."

"I'd heard about this old retired cop," Austin began, "who was nosing around trying to get a lead on Angie's killer, and I had to meet him. Seems he's somewhat of a legend around these parts. I heard his name more than once while they were questioning me over at the police station."

"I'm no legend," Charles objected. "I'm actually more of an annoyance. I can't seem to stay out of cases that are close to home, even though the department would like for me to."

"I've already told you how much I appreciate what you're doing, but the real reason I wanted to come over today," Austin said, turning to Sarah and Sophie, "was to thank you two for getting the name of that Caldwell guy. The cops were ready to charge me with the murder of Josh's girl before you gals came in with another suspect. How did you ever do that?"

Sarah and Sophie told Austin about their visit to Elkins and their meeting with Angie's friends.

"Clarissa?" he responded. "Nice kid. I always liked that girl. She was a good friend to Angie. I don't know the others, but I'm sure glad you went to see them. Charles here told me they'd sent a retired cop to talk to her friends and he didn't get anywhere. How did you gals get them to tell you so much?"

"I think they were just more comfortable with us. A couple of gray-haired grandmothers are much less intimidating than an undercover cop, retired or not," Sarah commented.

"I heard about that guy," Austin said with a chuckle. "He went into Elkins like some big-city cop, and everybody just shut down. Josh said he threw him out of the house when he came there interrogating him and his wife like he thought they had something to do with their little girl's death."

Sarah smiled at Austin's protective tone and said, "It sounds like you still thought of Angela as a little girl."

"I've known that girl since she was born. I waited with Josh after they tossed him out of the delivery room. Josh is production manager at the Landover Hills Energy Plant back home, and he's used to being in charge, but the doc pulled rank and sent him packing. Josh was angry, but I think he was mostly scared. Adelaide had a hard pregnancy and, as it turned out, they almost lost Angie. I think we all hung on to her pretty hard the rest of her life."

"Losing her must have been very hard on everyone," Charles concluded.

Austin stood and walked over to the window, but Sarah saw the tears in his eyes. "That girl was like a daughter to me. I taught her to play the guitar, but she brought that beautiful voice of hers herself. She sang in the choir and had the lead every year in her high school plays. Her music teacher told me they picked musicals every year so Angela could have the lead and the community could hear her sing." His voice cracked when he added, "The whole town came to those plays just to hear her."

"How long had she been singing with you?" Sophie asked.

Austin chuckled as he moved away from the window and faced his host. "The first time she was five years old," he said with a broad grin. "She was sitting with her family in the front row down in Tennessee. They always came to see me when they could. Anyway, my performance had just started, and I led off with one of Angie's favorites. She hopped right up out of that seat and ran up onto the stage. The security guy tried to catch her, but she was just too fast. Angie started singing before she even reached me, and then she stood right there next to me holding onto my pants leg and bellowed out that song like she'd been on the stage all her life. The crowd went wild!"

By the time he got to the end of his story, Austin was laughing, but tears were streaming down his cheeks. "Yeah," he said, "I loved that little gal, and she had a great career ahead of her. We were just discouraging it until she finished school."

"Did she go to school around here?" Sarah asked.

"No, she went to college back home. She came up here to help Grandma as soon as classes had ended for the summer. She was scheduled to head back next week." He dropped his eyes and sat quietly for a few moments. "She and I had been talking about a couple of years at Juilliard. She was good enough to get in, but we're talking at least $70,000 a year. I promised to finance it and was looking into backing her career. I make more money than I'll ever need, and that young lady would have been a winner for sure."

Then, shaking his head as if he could shake away the memories, he turned to Sophie. "So, Sophie," he said, picking up another slice of pizza and changing the subject, as men will often do when the conversation becomes too emotional, "I understand we practically went to school together."

Sophie laughed. "Well, we shared the same building, probably the same classrooms, and it wouldn't surprise me if we used some of the same library books, but you came along about forty years after me."

Austin chuckled. "I stopped by the old building the other day," he said. "Not much has changed. Did you know old Ed Hunt, the custodian?"

"Sure," she responded, looking pleased to hear his name. "Ed was in my class back in the day, but then he dropped out of school. Something happened, but I never knew what, and he disappeared for a while. Rumor had it that he was in prison, but I don't know that for sure," she added thoughtfully. "Then the year I graduated, he was back as the school custodian. He can't still be working there," she exclaimed with surprise, realizing the man would be near eighty himself.

"You bet, and he remembered me right away," Austin added, sounding amazed.

"Excuse me for stating the obvious, Austin," Sarah interjected, "but you're a hard person to forget. I'm reminded of you every time I turn the radio on."

"Good for you, gal," he added with a grin. "That means you're listening to good ol' American music, country style."

They visited for an hour or so more until the pizza was gone and Austin had caught Sophie up on many of the town's changes over the years. Charles brought in a couple more beers from the kitchen and suggested they move to the backyard. "We won't have many more of these nice warm afternoons."

"I think Sophie and I will get back to our sewing," Sarah said, knowing that Austin and Charles likely wished to discuss the case.

As the men stood and headed out of the room, Sarah noticed that Barney was watching Austin intently. The dog often attached himself to men wearing boots, and Sarah had always assumed they reminded him of the homeless men in the woods who had taken care of him until Sarah gave Barney his forever home. But, in this case, she burst out laughing as she suddenly understood his attraction to Austin. Barney had a whole slice of pizza dangling from his mouth and an innocent look on his face.

"When this dog becomes fat and lazy and refuses to eat dog food," she said jokingly to Austin, "you better be prepared to arrange his daily pizza delivery."

"The poor dog needs comfort foods just like we do," Sophie sputtered as she left the room. "Oh, I forgot to ask him about the concert," she said, abruptly turning to head back toward the living room.

"I think he has enough on his mind right now, Sophie. The department was about to charge him with Angela's murder before they found out about Nathan Caldwell. Let's let him spend some time relaxing with Charles."

"I love Austin's music," Sophie said thoughtfully as she got situated in her sewing chair, "but I had no idea what a nice guy he is—very gentle and kind. How could anyone think he could murder anyone? Just listen to his music. He's all about love."

"I agree, Sophie, but I must admit we don't really know the man. We know his music, and we've loved it, but we really don't know Austin Bailey, the man."

"Excuse me?" Sophie objected. "He's from my hometown, and I've been hearing about him since he was a teenager and singing in the local choir. Austin Bailey is a good boy and not a murderer. I can vouch for him personally!"

Sarah decided not to argue with her friend. Once Sophie's mind was made up, that was it.

"And," Sophie added defiantly, "if those cops don't get out there and find the real killer, I'll just have to do it myself."

* * * * *

"What time did Austin finally leave the other day?" Sophie asked as she and Sarah were sitting on a bench in the dog park watching Emma and Barney wrestle in the grass.

"He ended up staying for dinner. I had a pot roast in the Crock-Pot so I asked if he'd stay."

"Did he say anything else about Angela?"

"No, and I think he was happy to just hang around and enjoy a home-cooked meal and some mindless relaxation. The guys had a couple more beers, watched some baseball, and took Barney for a walk. I agree with you about the man, by the way. He's a kindhearted and caring person. Barney loves him dearly, but then I suspect there was some bribery involved in that relationship," she added with a raised eyebrow, remembering how often Barney had licked his lips as he sat under Austin's chair.

"I learned one thing last night that came as quite a surprise," Sarah continued.

"What's that?"

"Well, remember Charles said Austin had canceled his shows for the next few months so he could stay here until Angela's murder was resolved?"

"I remember. Has he changed his mind?"

"No, as it turns out, that's not the reason he's here. He's been told not to leave town."

"What? A famous man like Austin? Are they afraid he'll drop out of sight?" Sophie retorted sarcastically. "How do they think he could disappear? If you want to know where he is, you just do a computer search on his schedule."

"That's true, but what's worrying me about the whole thing is that he is still a prime suspect. And that especially worries me because it tells me they aren't seriously looking for anyone else."

"Is that what Charles says?" Sophie asked.

"No. He said the department continues to work all cases and follows up on any leads, but I just don't think that's entirely true. I'm sure they work much harder to find the killer when they don't have someone already in their sights. But once they have someone, who knows?"

"Makes sense," Sophie responded thoughtfully. "Maybe we need to do some undercover work, and I say we start with that nursing home. Surely someone saw something over there."

"You think they might be involved in her death?"

"No," Sophie replied. "I just think we need to talk to some of the staff and see if there is something they might have forgotten to tell the police. You know, like we did with

Angela's friends. No one would have ever known about the Caldwell guy if we hadn't stuck our noses in."

"Oh, on a lighter vein," Sarah said, "there's something else I wanted to tell you. During dinner the other night I started describing that incredible night sky that we experienced in Missouri, and Austin got all melancholy. He said he knows that starlit sky and has often sat under it on his grandparents' farm. He said that he composed some of his best music at night under that magnificent sky."

"You look a little pensive yourself, Sarah. Are you about to create a song?"

"Not a song, but I've been thinking about a quilt based on that sky. I thought maybe I could find a night sky fabric, maybe black, or maybe very dark blue."

"And the stars?" Sophie asked.

"I'll have to look it up, but I think somewhere I saw a block called the Missouri Star. It was in that book I had on the history of quilting. Maybe it was during the antebellum period? I'm not sure. I think I'll look it up."

"And you're thinking about making it?"

"I'm thinking about making it for Austin."

"What a lovely idea," Sophie acclaimed. "It would mean a great deal to him. He's lost so much this summer. ..."

The two women sat quietly watching the dogs run around the dog park, taking turns biting at each other's ankles playfully.

"So," Sophie finally said, straightening up on the bench and rolling her shoulders to get the stiffness out. "Let's talk about Peggy and her bruises. I think we should do something. What do you think?"

"I think we should wait until after the next meeting and then go see her."

"I disagree," Sophie responded. "It could be too late."

"Too late? Why 'too late'? What do you think is going to happen?"

"I don't know," Sophie replied, "but I have a bad feeling about it. I've been thinking about the bruises, the dark glasses, the missed meetings, then withdrawing from the club entirely. You know what this sounds like?"

"What?"

"It sounds to me like this woman is being abused. Who does she live with?"

"I actually don't know," Sarah responded thoughtfully. "I always assumed she wasn't married or maybe a widow. She's never mentioned a husband. I remember her talking to Delores one time, and Delores asked if she had children in the area."

"What did she say?"

"She said she didn't have children. She didn't say anything else about it and didn't mention a husband. You know how she talks, just one-word answers."

"Like she has something to hide?"

"Sophie, don't start creating a mystery where there isn't one. She just might be having falls. Maybe she needs to go to the doctor. We could help with that if she needed help."

"Okay, that means we need to go see her, and I'm in favor of going sooner rather than later. If you're right and she needs medical care, why wait?"

Sarah sighed. "I guess you're right. Whether she comes to the club or not, she's a member, and that's what we're there for. Not just to make quilts but to support each other and provide help when it's needed."

"Now you're talking!" Sophie declared. "I'll get the 3″ by 5″ card file box and …"

"Sophie!"

"Sorry."

They decided to go that afternoon. Sarah said she would pick Sophie up at 2:00 and they could stop by the quilt shop afterward and let Ruth know what they learned. However, things didn't go as smoothly as they had planned.

When they arrived at Peggy's house, they heard an angry male voice using foul language and apparently demanding something. He kept yelling, "Bring it to me now, you bitch."

Sarah and Sophie looked at one another inquisitively, each wondering if they should knock. "I hate to interrupt them," Sarah began.

"You'd hate to interrupt what's going on in there?" Sophie rebuffed sarcastically. "Personally, I think it needs to be interrupted. Besides, Peggy might be in danger."

They agreed to knock, but there was no answer. The hollering, however, stopped. Sophie knocked again. They heard someone walking near the door, and finally Peggy opened it just a crack and peeked out. "Yes?" she said, at first not recognizing them. But then she said, "Oh, Sarah and Sophie." She looked embarrassed and didn't seem to know what to do. She kept the door almost closed. "This isn't a good time," she finally said, and she closed the door. "I'm sorry," they heard her say after the door was closed.

"Was she saying that to him or to us, I wonder," Sophie reflected.

"I wonder what we should do," Sarah thought aloud.

"Call the police?" Sophie suggested

"We should talk to Charles. She didn't appear to be in imminent danger," Sarah said.

"Unless words can kill …" Sophie countered heatedly.

Chapter 11

"Have you told anyone else?" Charles asked as the three stood in the kitchen discussing their earlier encounter with Peggy.

"No," Sarah responded. "We had planned to stop and tell Ruth what we found out, but under the circumstances we didn't think it would be a good idea."

"Good decision. And there's a husband?"

"We don't know. I heard Peggy say she doesn't have kids, but she's never mentioned a husband one way or the other," Sophie replied.

"And you've seen bruises and a black eye?"

"Well, not exactly," Sarah explained about the bruise she saw on Peggy's back and the story Ruth had told about the sunglasses.

"That's not evidence of abuse," Charles proclaimed in his official tone.

"We know, Charles. But what we heard today was certainly abusive language. We just want to help her if she needs help, and she certainly seemed to need help."

"But did she seem to want help?" he asked.

"Maybe she's afraid," Sophie said, itching to take the 3″ by 5″ card file box out of her bag. She had brought it "just in case," she had said.

"The way it looks to me," Charles began in his most investigative tone, "is that someone is possibly abusing your friend. She may well need help, but it's just possible that she doesn't want it. That happens, you know. We see it all the time," he added, thinking back to his days on the force. "We'd go out and try to help and then all of a sudden the couple, battered and bleeding, swear eternal love and send us away, only to call a week later with new injuries. I'll never understand it."

"She needs our help, Charles, whether she can admit it or not."

"We need to talk about this rationally," Sophie interjected, seeing that her friends weren't getting anywhere. "Is it okay if I make a pitcher of iced tea, and we go sit down?"

"Of course. Thank you, Sophie," Sarah responded, feeling a little embarrassed that she hadn't thought of it herself. "And I'll get us a snack. How about crackers and cheese?"

"And something sweet," Sophie suggested as she started the teapot and reached for glasses.

"And a bowl of fresh fruit," Sarah added, always looking out for her husband's diet.

Sarah had no sooner set the tray of food in the center of the table when the telephone rang. "It's for you," Charles announced, bringing her the phone. "A Margaret Broadhurst," he added. "Do you know who that is?"

"No," Sarah responded, looking confused.

"Isn't that Peggy's last name? Broadhurst?" Sophie asked.

"I think it might be," Sarah replied, suddenly recognizing it. She took the phone and nodded her acknowledgment that it was, in fact, Peggy. She didn't put it on speaker, so the other two didn't get much of an idea of what the call was about, since Sarah mostly said, "That's not necessary," followed by "I understand. I understand."

They then heard her say, "Of course. That would be fine. Do you know where I live?" and there was a short pause. "Yes, we're a couple of blocks beyond there. Just keep going past the nursing home and the community center and turn right onto Sycamore Court. It's a cul-de-sac, and we're at the very end. The house is light green with dark green shutters—the only green house on the block. You can't miss it." Another pause. "Oh, of course. It's 112. Okay, we'll be watching for you," Sarah said, glancing up at Sophie and suddenly adding, "Peggy, are you still there? Good. I just wanted to tell you that Sophie is here...." She listened and smiled as she nodded in Sophie's direction. "I agree. We'll see you soon."

"So, I want the whole story," Sophie began, "but first I want to know what the two of you agree on that has to do with me."

"We agreed that you're a very nice lady and that we'd both be very pleased if you are here when she comes."

"And why is she coming?" Charles asked. "And how does she feel about me being here as well?"

"I decided not to ask her that. I want you to hear her story firsthand."

"Story?" Sophie asked, still not sure what was happening.

"She wants to explain what was going on when we were at her door."

"Did she give you any idea what it's all about?" Charles asked.

"No, but she seemed embarrassed about what we heard when we were at her door. I'm sure she wants to explain, but she also sounded like she really needs to talk to someone. She sounded worried, almost frightened. When she asked to come here, I was relieved. I was afraid we were going to have a hard time getting her to talk, but she seems eager."

"People always want to talk to you about their problems, Sarah," Charles said, pouring himself another glass of tea.

"As I recall," Sarah reminded him with a half-grin, "you were one of those people when we first met." Their first meeting had been in the coffee shop of the community center. Charles, following a massive stroke and a lengthy recovery period, had just moved into an independent living arrangement in the community. Sarah was a volunteer at the nursing home and had been assigned as his friendly visitor. At first, Sarah was reluctant to accept the assignment, as all of her previous clients had been women in the nursing home. But the moment they met, they realized they had met before. Conversation flowed comfortably between them, and they decided to turn down the formal arrangement and simply do things together as friends.

"It's because she listens," Sophie interjected in response to Charles' comment. "That's why people tell her their problems. You can tell she's listening. She stops whatever she's doing and gives you her total attention. She doesn't just nod her head occasionally like most folks do, and she doesn't say stupid things like, 'Oh, don't feel that way, Sophie.' She really listens, and people need that, especially folks around here."

Charles, already seated at the table, nodded his agreement without looking up from the newspaper he had picked up.

"Like you're doing," Sophie added with annoyance.

"Oh, sorry," Charles said, laying the paper down.

Sarah fussed around the kitchen for a few minutes, getting things in order, but then stopped and looked at Sophie. "This room feels a little crowded. Do you think Peggy would be more comfortable in the living room, or would that feel too formal?"

"How about the backyard?" Charles suggested. "I could open a bottle of wine, and we could put more cheese and crackers out. That way, if it seems like she wants to talk more privately, I can just move away from the table and pull a few weeds or something."

Sarah laughed. "That sounds a little contrived, but let's go with it. It would certainly be a more relaxed setting, and she just might feel like talking. We don't know if she drinks, so I'll bring the tea pitcher as well." By the time they were all set up in the backyard, they could hear a car pulling into the driveway.

Sarah went out the side gate and met Peggy as she was getting out of her car. "We're in the backyard having a glass of wine. If it's okay with you, we'll just sit out there."

"It sounds perfect. We won't be having many more days like this with fall right around the corner. And, I'll have to admit, that glass of wine sounds like just what I need."

Charles had brought a couple of canvas lounge chairs out, and Peggy, after being introduced to Charles, headed straight for one of the chairs. "Ah," she said. "Relaxation at last."

Charles reached for a glass and the wine bottle and held them in the air in Peggy's direction with his eyebrows raised.

"Absolutely," she asserted. "Thank you."

Charles was surprised when he realized that Peggy was much younger than he had expected. "Do you live here in the community?" he asked.

"No, but I'm just a few miles from here. I live on the other side of the park, closer to the river." Charles knew the area, as he often walked Barney on over to the river after their visits to the dog park.

"My son lives over there," Sophie said. "He's on Braddock. In fact, Sarah's daughter lives there too. Did you know that my son is married to Sarah's daughter?"

"Yes," Peggy responded, suddenly remembering the connection. "I had forgotten about that, but now I remember you talking about it last year. How's your daughter enjoying being a new mom?" she asked, turning to Sarah.

"She's taken to it like a fish to water," Sarah said, laughing. "You must have been at the quilt club when we were all talking about her fear of becoming a mother to a fourteen-year-old daughter, but it's just what they both needed. Martha needed a daughter to fuss over, and Penny sure needed a mother."

"That's right. Her mother died, didn't she?"

"Yes," Sophie responded. "And that's when Timothy brought his daughter home, and I officially became a grandmother."

The next ten minutes or so were filled with small talk, no one ready to address the real issue. Finally, wanting to make it easier for Peggy, Sarah broached the subject by saying,

"You had us worried earlier, Peggy. Sophie and I were afraid you needed some kind of help and were afraid to ask."

"I need help, but not in the way you mean."

"How can we help?" *Open-ended questions*, Sarah reminded herself. That was something she had learned in her volunteer orientation. *Don't ask a question that can be answered with one word.*

"It's my husband, Leon."

Ah, so there's a husband, the others thought simultaneously and glanced at one another.

"What's going on, Peggy?" Sarah asked gently as she moved over to sit in the empty chair next to her.

"He wasn't always like this. Leon and I've been married for thirty-five years, and they were good years up until recently." She hesitated and seemed to be looking back over the years. "Well," she continued, "I guess that's not quite true. The truth is they haven't been good for quite a while. You see, Leon was diagnosed with Alzheimer's a few years ago."

"I thought they couldn't diagnose Alzheimer's except during an autopsy," Sophie said.

"That used to be true," Peggy agreed, "but modern medicine has made early diagnosis easier. Leon went through all the tests—physical and neurological exams, MRI and CT scans. The doctor said the tests were to rule out other causes of dementia. They started him on a medication that they said might slow down the progression. I don't know whether it did or not."

"But what about the way he was talking to you when we were at your house?" Sophie asked. "Has he always been so abusive?"

Peggy seemed taken aback by Sophie's directness but thought about it for a moment before answering. "Leon has always been strong-willed, and he always made the final decisions in our marriage when we disagreed. But I wouldn't call him abusive. He never struck me, at least not back then, if that's what you mean."

"How has he changed?" Charles asked.

"At first we thought it was just normal aging stuff. You know, forgetting things. But it changed. He started having problems figuring things out—things he'd always been able to do, like change the oil in the car, put a piece of furniture together. He used to do our taxes himself, but a few years ago he just stuffed all the paperwork in a drawer and didn't even attempt them."

"That must have been hard for you," Sarah said.

"It was, but I kept thinking it was normal. But then it got to a point where he would lose something and angrily accuse me of hiding it." Peggy handed her empty glass to Charles and said, "May I?"

"Of course," Charles commented. "I should have noticed you needed a refill. I was just engrossed in your story."

Peggy took a sip of her wine and continued. "Last year it became much worse. He went into what the doctor called the combative stage. He just became filled with rage and would lash out at me. He seemed to be blaming me for what was happening to him."

"Lashing out physically?" Charles asked.

"Physically, verbally—any way he could. Later he wouldn't even seem to remember that he'd done it. Like this morning," she added, looking at Sarah and Sophie. "After you left he put his arm around me and asked when we were leaving. I don't know where he thought we were going, but he clearly had no idea how terrible he had treated me ten minutes before that. But then when I was leaving to come over here, he didn't seem to know who I was."

"Where is he now? Can you leave him alone?" Sophie asked.

"I hate to impose on her, but I ask my neighbor to sit on the front porch just to make sure he doesn't leave the house. I don't go far, and I have her call me if he tries to leave, and I rush back home to deal with it. I don't want him hurting anyone else."

"So he's wandered off?"

"Oh yes. I had to call the police twice, but he was found both times over in the park. He always loved going there, and he somehow found his way."

"So this explains why you stopped coming to the quilt club," Sarah said.

"And it explains the bruises and sunglasses," Sophie added.

Peggy looked mortified. "People know?" she exclaimed and began to sob.

"It's okay," Sarah said as she put her arms around Peggy in an attempt to comfort her as she shot a disapproving look in Sophie's direction.

"Sorry," Sophie said contritely. "I can see how that wasn't the thing to say. I'm sorry, Peggy. And as far as I know, no one else knows about it. Just us. Sarah noticed the bruises once and Ruth mentioned the sunglasses, but your friends are just concerned about you."

"I'm so ashamed," Peggy whispered.

"Peggy, this isn't your fault," Sarah insisted. "Your husband is sick, and you both need help. Have you spoken to anyone about getting help in the house?"

"No, I don't think he would want someone else around."

"Peggy, it's time for you to begin making the big decisions. He isn't able to make them any longer. You need help. I'll get some numbers for you," Sarah offered. "The Alzheimer's Association certainly can refer you to home health aides who are trained in working with folks with dementia."

"I have a friend here in the village that goes to a caregivers' support group," Sophie said, still regretting how much she had upset Peggy with her comment. "My friend says it has saved her sanity. She said it's reassuring to spend time talking with people who are going through the same things she is. You probably don't know this, but my husband had Alzheimer's as well."

"He did?" Peggy said, looking surprised.

"Yes, but before we moved here, he fell down two flights of stairs. He forgot where he was and tumbled all the way down. He broke his back and ended up in a nursing home. His dementia progressed rapidly, and he never got out of the nursing home. He was transferred to the Memory Care Unit right here in the village after I sold the house and moved here. I was able to visit him every day, but it wasn't like it is for you since he wasn't living with me during the advanced stages."

She told the story in a very matter-of-fact tone, but Sarah knew she was protecting herself from giving in to the emotion that surrounded that period of her life. Sarah knew it took a great deal of strength for her to share her story, but she also knew that her friend had told it for Peggy's benefit.

"I went to that support group too, even after he was gone." Sophie looked away and passed her empty glass to Charles.

"I'm really falling down on the job," he muttered.

The conversation became less intense as the four sipped wine and munched on the additional cheese and crackers that Sarah had added to the tray. When Peggy announced that she had to get back home, they quickly went over what they had decided to do. Sophie promised to call with the phone number of the support group, and Sarah was going to make an appointment and take Peggy to meet with a counselor at the local Alzheimer's Association.

"I'd be happy to sit with him when you meet with them," Charles volunteered. "Perhaps he would like to walk over to the dog park with Barney and me."

"He'd like that," Peggy responded, "but don't forget that he can be a handful."

"These are retired cop hands," Charles replied, holding his hands up. "They can handle anything."

"And have," Sarah added, thinking of some of the stories he had told her about breaking up barroom brawls.

Once everyone had left, Sarah sat back down in the backyard and looked over at her husband.

He shook his head and said, "Well, that's another nice mess you've gotten us into, Stanley," quoting his favorite philosophers.

"Isn't it a *fine* mess, not a *nice* mess?" Sarah corrected. "That's another fine mess you've gotten us into?"

"Nope. Laurel and Hardy never said, 'That's another fine mess.' They were misquoted by the newspapers. However, their 1930s movie was, in fact, named *Another Fine Mess*."

"You're just a wealth of information, my dear husband."

* * * * *

Lying in bed and listening to the gentle snore of her husband, Sarah's mind traveled back to Peggy, and she wondered what it would be like to have her husband not recognize her nor remember the life they'd had together. Peggy said sometimes Leon would remember things from many years in the past, but Sarah and Charles had only been together for the last five years. *What would he remember?*

A ninety-year-old woman who Sarah had visited in the Memory Care Unit had once told Sarah that she had to leave now, because her mother wanted her home before dark. Sarah remembered noticing that the woman wasn't upset about it and had no idea that her reality had moved back eighty-some years into the past.

"And they say time travel isn't possible," she thought but must have said aloud because Charles responded.

"What did you say, dear?" he muttered, changing his position on the bed and sighing deeply as he drifted back to sleep. Sarah smiled and sent up a little prayer of thanks for the incredible people she had in her life.

Chapter 12

The next morning when Sarah returned from her assignments at the nursing home, she found Charles sitting at the kitchen table, deeply engrossed in his new laptop. Sarah was feeling the need to be alone anyway, so she headed for the sewing room and pulled out the two additional placemats she had made earlier in the week using some leftover half-square triangles she had found in her scrap bag.

The tops were finished, and they had been turned, stitched, and pressed. All they needed were a few lines of quilting, and she had decided to try out some of her special stitches. She chose a stitch that formed a row of small flowers and created diagonal lines of stitches every few inches using a contrasting thread. The hum of the machine lulled her into a meditative state, and she could feel the stress melting away.

What did I do before I had quilting, she wondered, and immediately she felt herself transposed to the garden behind the home where she had raised her children. At the end of the day, she would pull on her gardening clothes and lovingly nurture her plants for an hour or so as the sun prepared to set. It was during those hours that she found peace after the children's father died. When she moved to the retirement village, she had worried about leaving her garden, but quilting had quickly taken its place.

She wondered if that was how Angela Padilla had felt about her own secret garden.

* * * * *

Sarah and Sophie had spent too much time poking through the fabrics on the sale table at Running Stitches and were late getting to the club meeting in the back room. Ruth smiled at them as they took their seats and continued talking. "Several volunteers are coming by later this evening from Meals on Wheels to pick up the placemats and to meet the folks who made them. I wish more of us could have been here," she added as she looked around the room at the sparse attendance, "but it's the last week of summer, and I guess our friends are taking advantage of the nice weather."

"Actually, several of our quilters are shopping for school clothes at the mall sale," Christina said.

"That's right. I forgot about the back-to-school sale. I guess those of us who are here don't have to worry about school clothes anymore."

"Or packing lunches," Kimberly added.

"Or getting kids to the bus on time ..."

"I miss those days," Becky said, sounding melancholy. "Those were happy days."

"Okay, folks. You're becoming maudlin again," Sophie announced. She wasn't one for sentimentality. "Forget the soppiness and let's get on with the show."

Ruth laughed and continued. "Okay, so these women will be here in about an hour, and I was hoping we could fill the time until they get here with our show-and-tell. Does anyone have anything to share with us?"

Kimberly and her sister Christina stood and unfolded a large scrap quilt they had just finished quilting on their long-arm machine. "We didn't buy one piece of material for this quilt," Kimberly bragged. "It all came out of the scrap bag." The group applauded their ingenuity and asked questions about the pattern. Christina reached into her tote bag and pulled out a Bonnie Hunter book on making scrap quilts and said, "This woman can do miracles with scrap."

"Anyone else?" Ruth asked.

No one spoke up until Sophie started poking Sarah and saying, "Show them."

"I'm really not ready …"

"Oh, go on. They might have some ideas for the problem you were telling me about."

"Show us," everyone started saying until Sarah sighed and reached for her bag.

"Okay, but I'm really not ready. I'm still thinking about this project." She pulled out a pile of embroidered vintage dresser scarves. "These belonged to my mother and her sister. I think some of them might have been made by their mother, but, unfortunately, no one knows for sure." She passed them both ways around the table, and the quilters examined them, admiring the work and speculating about what could be done with them.

She then pulled out the two blocks she had completed. She had framed the embroidered section within a narrow Churn Dash design—green in one block and blue in the other. Caitlyn, who had joined the meeting late and explained that she had actually gone to the sale at the mall but decided she'd rather be with the quilters, frowned and said, "But that would mean you had to cut them up."

"I struggled with that point, Caitlyn, but I decided that they aren't doing anyone any good bundled up in this box, and no one in my family is going to put them out on their tables, so why not preserve the handwork in a quilt."

"Hmm," Caitlyn responded thoughtfully. "I guess you're right. That would bring them back to life, wouldn't it?" Everyone sat quietly for a few moments letting that thought sink in.

Bring them back to life, Sarah pondered. *That's exactly what I want to do.*

"This is going to be a unique tribute to the women in your family who spent their time making these tiny little embroidery stitches to form these beautiful pieces of vintage art," Kimberly offered. "As Caitlyn said, you're bringing them back to life."

"More schmaltz," Sophie said so softly that only Sarah heard her.

The evening ended on a much more serious note. The three women who came to pick up the placemats first told wonderful stories about the Meals on Wheels service and how appreciative the recipients were when they brought their meals. All three admitted that they often sat and visited for a few minutes because the people were so alone and in need of human contact.

That led to the telling of some rather sad stories. The quilters sat quietly, picturing the elderly woman who could only transfer herself a few feet from her bed to her chair to her portable commode and back. Or the man who they found on the floor on a Monday. He had fallen on Friday and lain there all weekend. "I had to climb in through the window," his volunteer added.

"They are always so glad to see us come," continued the volunteer, "and it never seems to be the food that they are happy to see. It always breaks my heart to leave them."

"Don't these people have any family?" Christina asked.

"Apparently not," the oldest of the three women said. "If they did, I assume they wouldn't be so alone."

"That's not necessarily true," Delores said sorrowfully. "There are older folks in our retirement community who never see their family. Families just aren't like they used to be. The kids grow up and move away. I have two grand-children I've never even met. Of course, they live out of the country, but still, families just don't mean what they did when I was young."

Getting the evening back on a more positive note, Ruth began unpacking the placemats and spreading them out on the table. The visitors starting excitedly choosing particular ones for certain people.

"Mary would love this one. She's always talking about her cat. ... And look at this one! Bertha loves her sweets, and this one has cherry pies all over it."

"I'm going to pull this one out right now for Mr. Schmidt. It's very masculine looking, and those others are too fussy for him."

"Here's another one that's great for a man," the woman said, holding up the one Sarah had made with horse fabric.

Turning to the group, Elizabeth, who appeared to be the leader of the three, said, "We can't begin to tell you how much we appreciate this. These beautiful placemats are going to bring so much joy to our clients."

Caitlyn and Allison helped the women load the boxes into their van, and when they returned to the room, both girls announced that they were going to volunteer. "They said I can start right away," Allison said, "and Caitlyn is going to do it during the summers when she comes home."

Sarah saw Caitlyn's face fall and her eyes cloud over for just a moment, but then she pulled herself together and joined in Allison's excitement.

"We need to get Caitlyn aside and find out what's going on with her," Sarah whispered to Sophie. "I don't like what I've been seeing lately."

Chapter 13

"Hi, Aunt Sarah," Caitlyn said as she answered the phone. She had called Sarah "aunt" from the day she came to live with her father in the village. Sarah felt it had to do with the girl having no family other than Andy. When Caitlyn was fourteen, her mother had disappeared and her stepfather had thrown her out of his house, so she lived on the streets for many months, surviving as best she could. Sarah and Sophie were instrumental in finding the girl and uniting her with the father she had never known.

Andy and his friends made a case for allowing the young girl to live in the retirement village, and she had become very attached to his close friends, particularly Sarah, Sophie, and Sophie's granddaughter Penny.

"Hi, Caitlyn. I just realized you'll be leaving for California soon, and I was hoping you'd have time to come have lunch with me before you leave."

There was a brief pause before the young girl replied, "I'd love that. How's today? Or is that too soon?" she quickly added.

"That's actually perfect. Charles is taking a woodworking class at the community center, and we'll have the house to ourselves. Come around noon?"

"I'll be there," Caitlyn responded, sounding more animated than she had at the beginning of the call.

Now what shall I fix? Sarah wondered. She was accustomed to cooking for Charles, with an eye toward his low-fat diet, but she didn't think what she usually prepared would be especially enjoyed by a teenager. *On the other hand, she's always worried about her weight, so maybe the usual fare is just fine*, Sarah told herself.

But ultimately she decided to take advantage of the opportunity to indulge in juicy hamburgers made with beef instead of turkey and savor the smell of french fries sizzling away in her long-abandoned deep fryer. Since she had plenty of time, she began by cutting up apples to make a pie from scratch.

"It's unlikely that my new school clothes will fit after this meal, Aunt Sarah," Caitlyn moaned after her second piece of pie. "Would it be okay to take a piece for Papa?"

"You certainly may. You can take several pieces, in fact. I don't want more than one piece left for Charles," Sarah said as she reached for a container. "I've always wondered about something," she said as she was scooping up the pie. "How come you call your father Papa? I was there the day you met him, and you said it then."

"It was a book I read when I was young, maybe eight or nine. My mother was married to a very cold, angry man. I always knew he hated me ..."

"Oh, Caitlyn, I'm sure he didn't hate you," Sarah interrupted.

"Oh, I'm sure of it. He told me so every day, and don't forget he threw me right out the door when Mama left. Anyway, I had this book about a girl who lived with her father. There was no mother. I don't remember why, but I was so envious of that girl. Her father was very kind and loving, and she called him Papa. I always dreamed of having a papa."

"And now you do!"

"And now I do," Caitlyn replied with a smile. But then her smile began to fade, and her eyes became clouded. "And now I'm leaving."

"Ah," Sarah replied knowingly. "That explains that look you've had lately, and you have right now as a matter of fact. You're worried about being away from Andy, your papa."

"Why did I do this, Aunt Sarah? There are perfectly good schools near here. I could live at home or at least come home on the weekends. I'm going to miss him so much, and I'm going to worry about him …"

"I know," Sarah responded as she wrapped her arms around the girl. She thought about the younger version who had slept in alleys and eaten in food kitchens, alone and on the street. Sarah realized she had been giving Caitlyn too much credit. She was still a young girl who had grown up without love and care. She was capable of independence and could certainly take care of herself. But she was still frightened inside.

"Do you think it's too late to change my mind?" she asked pleadingly.

"It's not too late, but if you truly want my advice …"

"I do. I trust you, Aunt Sarah."

That statement felt like a heavy burden, but Sarah poured out from her heart. "I think you need to face your fears and go on to college as planned. You have a safe place to live there with your father's aunt. Sophie and I will take excellent care of your papa until you come home. You don't have to commit to the full four years. You can go for one year and transfer if it isn't working for you, but I'm afraid you'll regret it if you don't go. We all have fears. The trick is to not let your fears make your decisions."

"You're wise, Aunt Sarah." Caitlyn was still bundled up in Sarah's arms and had wrapped her own arms around Sarah. They stood like that for a few more moments.

"I'd better get going," the young girl finally said. "I promised Penny I'd stop by this afternoon."

"She's going to miss you. You have my cell phone number, don't you?" Sarah asked, and Caitlyn assured her she had programmed everyone's number in.

"Call me anytime you want to talk, sweetie. You know I love you."

"I know," she responded, looking a bit embarrassed. "I love you too."

The house seemed unusually empty after Caitlyn left. "It was nice having a young person in the house," Sarah said aloud, and Barney came running to see if she had said something about leftover hamburger.

"This house smells like a truck stop," Charles exclaimed as he came into the kitchen from the garage a few hours later. "I hope that's my dinner."

"You know better, but I saved you a large piece of freshly baked apple pie, and you can have a scoop of real ice cream as my apology for making you deal with the smell. Frying seems to penetrate everything."

"You fried?"

"Yes, I dug the old deep fryer out of the garage and made a meal we'll call A Teenager's Delight."

"Did you two have a nice time?" he asked, already digging into his scrumptious treat.

"We had a good time and a good talk." Sarah proceeded to tell him about Caitlyn's concerns, and he agreed with the advice Sarah had given her.

Charles hadn't eaten the apple pie with the gusto Sarah expected, and he pushed the plate aside without finishing the last few bites.

"Is something wrong?" Sarah asked as she poured the oil from the pot into an empty coffee can.

"I stopped by the department this afternoon and saw Hal. There's been a development."

The concern in his voice caused Sarah to stop what she was doing and look at her husband.

"And?"

"Austin Bailey disappeared."

"Disappeared?" Sarah exclaimed. "What do you mean?"

"He just up and left town."

"Doesn't he have the right to do that?"

"It's not wise. He's a person of interest in a murder investigation."

"But he's not guilty," she declared.

"That's not what the department thinks."

"Is Hal upset?"

"Livid," was her husband's only response as he shook his head and sighed.

Chapter 14

"What are you working on so studiously over there?" Sophie asked as the two women sat in Sarah's sewing room a few days later, with Sophie's machine whirring away and Sarah's head bent down over a sheet of graph paper.

"I'm designing the quilt I was telling you about the other day, the one using the Missouri Star blocks. The one I'm making for Austin."

"Assuming he ever comes back," Sophie declared.

"Oh, he'll come back, Sophie. I feel certain he had a good reason for leaving. Of course, that's not what the police think."

"They think he's guilty?"

"Yes, that's what Charles says they've concluded. Hal says that he ran because he's guilty, but you and I know that can't be true. He must have had a good reason. I'm not sure how I know that, but I truly believe it."

"So do I," Sophie responded. "What about Charles?"

"He's wearing his cop hat more and more these days, but every time you and I come back from visiting the nursing home, he always asks if we learned anything. I think he's hoping for something that points away from Austin."

"So, show me what you've designed for the Missouri Star quilt you plan on making for Austin."

Sarah moved over to Sophie's worktable, which was apparently becoming a permanent fixture in her sewing room. She sat down by Sophie and opened her notebook. "Now this is the Missouri Star quilt block. See how the center is surrounded by triangles that work their way out to form eight points?" Sophie nodded, and Sarah continued, "I'm going to use two coordinated fabrics on each star." Turning to the second page, she said, "And this is the whole quilt—rows of stars separated by sashing cut from the same background material so that the stars will appear to be floating in the sky."

"It sounds beautiful, but you know I'm not far enough along with my quilting to be able to picture it finished. Will this be a bed quilt?" Sophie asked, studying the star block.

"It could be, but I think I'll make it throw size for Austin—something he can travel with if he wants to."

"Good idea," Sophie agreed with little enthusiasm.

"Don't you like the idea?"

"Of course I do, Sarah. It's just …"

"What?"

"What if he won't be traveling anymore? What if he ends up in prison? I'm really worried about him."

"We have to be positive, Sophie. I'm sure this is going to work out. Austin is a good man and an innocent man. This will work out. It has to," she added. "But right now what we need is fabric."

"Great," Sophie responded, happy to be changing the subject. "We're off to Running Stitches."

"Well, actually, that's how I made us late for our quilt meeting the other night. I was searching for just the right star fabric, and I don't think Ruth has what I'm looking for."

"And that is?" Sophie asked.

"I want something sparkly and appropriate for a night sky. I think perhaps something with silver."

"I doubt you'll ever find that at Stitches. I've never seen Ruth offering metallic prints," Sophie mentioned.

"So I think we have a trip to Hamilton in our future," Sarah announced.

Sophie clapped excitedly. "Oh good," she squealed. "I haven't been to any of the quilt shops in Hamilton. Didn't Kimberly say there are two or three?"

"There are two in town and one way out on the north side of town, probably two hours from here. Let's start with the two in town and then we can go from there."

"Oh, wait," Sophie said, looking serious. "Don't you have nursing home visits tomorrow?"

"Yes, so how about Thursday?"

* * * * *

"There's nothing here that reminds me of the night sky we saw in Missouri," Sarah grumbled. They were in the third quilt shop, which was outside of town, having had no luck at the two shops in Hamilton.

"You just want it to represent the sky, right?" Sophie confirmed. "I saw this star fabric over here," she said as she walked back to a previous shelf, "but these are actually printed-on stars and clouds. That's not what you're looking for, is it? I noticed you just gave it an indifferent glance when you walked by."

"Right. I don't want the background to be a night sky—just to represent one."

"How about this solid black?"

"Too severe."

"Or this one?" Sophie asked, holding up a black-and-gray mottled fabric. "The gray sort of looks like clouds."

"True," Sarah agreed reluctantly, with a vague feeling that the mood wasn't quite right.

They were looking through the tone-on-tones, attempting to find the perfect sky, when Sarah sighed and said, "Let's look for star fabrics. I want to find two fabrics to use in all of the Missouri Stars, a light and a medium. I already know the background will be dark."

They pulled out several bolts of shimmery fabrics and auditioned them against a tone-on-tone navy blue that temporarily stood in for the background sky fabric. "I like it," Sarah said hesitantly, "but something is missing."

They each combed the shop on their own for a while, but neither one found fabric that particularly struck Sarah as that one perfect fabric line for her stars.

She was beginning to feel discouraged when she suddenly heard Sophie squeal. "How about these?" Sophie yelled from the pre-cut section as she waved a bundle of squares in the air. Sarah was astounded. The fabrics appeared to be twinkling.

"Let me see those up close," she called out excitedly as she hurried across the room. She examined the contents of the packet and said, "Oh, these are perfect."

"Why does it say it's a layer cake?" Sophie asked, examining the label.

"A layer cake is a bundle of ten-inch squares, usually from one fabric line. It looks like there are forty-two in this set."

"All different?" Sophie asked.

"It looks like there are two of each in this bundle, so twenty-one different fabrics."

"This won't work for you then," Sophie said emphatically as she started to put it back on the table. "You wanted to just use two fabrics."

"Wait! I'm flexible," Sarah said with a Cheshire cat grin as she reached for the bundle. "I'll make it scrappy." Sarah thumbed through the bundle and saw that there was an even distribution of lights and darks, and they were actually all very similar. "This will work," she said excitedly. "Just look at how it sparkles!"

"Look over here," Sophie shouted. "There's yardage of the same fabric."

"Looks like you've found a border and a back for me," Sarah exclaimed as she hurried over and picked out two of the bolts. They headed for the cutting table, excitedly debating which fabric should be the border and which should be the back.

"Do you know how to make the Missouri Star block?" Sophie asked as they were leaving the shop.

"I have the picture that I showed you, but I think I'll do a computer search and see if I can find any shortcuts online. I'm concerned about all the bias edges." Sophie, being new to quilting, asked about bias edges, and on the way home Sarah explained some of the problems and solutions.

"What about the sky?" Sophie asked as they were approaching Middletown.

"We'll deal with that another day."

"Soon?"

"It will have to be soon since the background is part of the block and I can't begin without it, but that's it for today."

"But I think we need to drive by Stitches. I remember a bolt on the sale rack that I think might be just what you're looking for." Sarah smiled as she thought about how much progress Sophie had made in the short time since she'd begun quilting. She'd always been interested in crafts and needlework, so it wasn't too much of a stretch for her to become a quilter.

"Do you want to go there now?" Sarah asked, and Sophie enthusiastically said yes.

As Sarah was pulling into a parking spot in front of the quilt shop, Sophie began reaching into the back seat for the bag of fabric.

"Don't bother with that," Sarah began, but Sophie interrupted.

"Don't you want to take these in and show them to Ruth?"

"I feel a little guilty about buying from another shop," Sarah admitted. "Let's just take a look at the bolt you saw."

"But I think you need to compare it with your star fabrics," Sophie said, and Sarah realized her friend was right. She took the bag from Sophie, and they headed into the shop.

"It looks good," Sophie was saying as Ruth walked up.

"Oh, I love that fabric," Ruth exclaimed, reaching for the sparkling bundle. "Where did you find it?" Sarah was embarrassed to admit she'd been shopping at Ruth's competitors, but her friend didn't appear to be in the least offended and, in fact, asked if she could write down the name of the line. "I'd love to offer this in the shop."

The three women agreed that the fabric Sophie had found, a very dark blue with a subtle tone-on-tone design of various-size dots, would make a perfect night sky. "The dots look like distant stars and planets," Sophie suggested as they headed for the cutting table.

"It's time to go home," Sarah announced, suddenly realizing she was exhausted from a very long day of shopping.

Chapter 15

"Austin left a message on our machine while we were out this morning," Charles said as he walked into the sewing room and sat down on the futon. They had just returned from the gym, and Sarah was settled into her sewing room, dividing her new fabrics into piles of lights, mediums, and darks. She was pleased to see that the darkest star fabrics were still lighter than her very dark-blue sky fabric.

"That's good news, isn't it?" Sarah asked, confused by her husband's lack of enthusiasm.

"He simply said that he had something to do and that he'd be back as soon as he could. He asked for me to cover for him with the department," Charles added with a deep sigh.

"What does that mean?" Sarah asked, looking puzzled.

"I have no idea." Charles didn't look pleased, and Sarah knew the request put him in an awkward position.

"Are you going to tell Hal?"

"I haven't told him yet. I don't know."

"You have to tell him."

"I'm not so sure, Sarah. He would have called Hal if he wanted the police to know what he's doing. He called me, and he asked for a favor. I like the guy, Sarah ..."

"And you're a retired cop," she rebutted. "You know you have to tell the department about this. And what did he mean when he asked you to cover for him?"

"I don't know what he had in mind, but I'll figure out what to do. Let's just let it drop for now."

"Let it drop?" Sarah exclaimed, but Charles had already left the room. He looked worried, and she decided it would be best to leave him alone. She knew from experience that he would seclude himself in his den for a while and come out eventually with a smile and a plan.

A couple of hours later, Sarah fixed lunch and tapped lightly on the door to Charles' den before opening it and telling him lunch was ready.

"I'm not hungry, hon," he responded. Sarah sat down and waited for him to say more. "I called Hal," he said finally. "I wasn't going to tell him about the phone call from Austin, but he was talking like the department thinks he's running because he's afraid they're going to arrest him. I figured it was best for me to tell him exactly what Austin told me— that he had something to take care of and he'll be back as soon as he can."

"What did Hal say?"

"Nothing. He just grunted," Charles said with a less-than-amused chuckle.

"Has Austin broken any laws by leaving town?" Sarah asked. "I know they told him not to."

Charles chuckled again despite his dark mood. "No, actually that's something you'll see in the movies and on television—even in books—but not in reality. The department has no authority to tell anyone not to leave town. The court can say that when a guy's out on bail, but not when it's just a person of interest who hasn't been charged with a crime."

"But Austin said he couldn't leave town," Sarah explained.

"He may have heard it that way, but it's more likely they requested that he be available in case they have more questions."

"So it doesn't really matter that he left town, does it?" Sarah asked hopefully.

"It matters because of the signal it sends to the department. It makes the guy look guilty, and that's exactly what Hal is thinking right now. He feels they have their sights on the killer."

"How could they think that? There's no possible motive."

"Well, actually Hal said the detective in charge of the investigation is pretty convinced that Austin did have a motive."

"And what possible motive would that be?" Sarah asked with her fists indignantly planted on her hip bones.

"Jealousy. Perhaps a love triangle," he suggested.

"That's crazy, Charles. The girl is nearly half his age, and he's known her since she was born. He loved her, but he was certainly not *in* love with her," Sarah huffed.

"Well …" Charles replied, dragging out his words. "That might not be entirely true. Rumors were really flying among the band members and the roadies working with them."

"What do you mean?" Sarah demanded, her face becoming flushed. "Rumors about what?"

"About Angie and Austin. No one had any specifics, but everyone just assumed they were a couple."

"Well, that's not proof of anything, and you heard how he described her when he was here. He bragged about the fact that she called him Uncle Austin and how he was always included in their family functions. I'm sure he loved her, but I can't believe it was what those people were thinking."

"I agree with you, Sarah," Charles responded. "I totally agree with you, but that doesn't change how the police look at it."

They sat quietly for a few minutes, each lost in thought. Sarah finally asked, "But if the police believe he was in love with her, then why do they think he would kill her? I still don't see a motive."

"One of the guys in the band had been making moves on her," Charles began, but Sarah immediately interrupted him.

"That's not a reason to kill her … the guy, maybe, but not her."

"The department doesn't see it that way. They hear rumors of an affair, probably started by this guy, and they begin speculating that there was a love relationship gone sour and that Austin killed her in a fit of anger."

"Oh, in a fit of anger," Sarah refuted sarcastically, "he went out and purchased a poison and used it to kill the woman he loved? That's pretty illogical even for the police department." The words had no sooner left her mouth when she realized they were hurtful. The department had been Charles' life for many years, and he took his job seriously. "I'm sorry, Charles," she added. "I didn't mean that. I'm just frustrated by this whole thing. I wish Austin were here."

"He'd probably be arrested if he was," Charles responded.

"Oh my," Sarah said with a sigh, shaking her head. "Charles, we've got to do something to help this man."

"I know, sweetie. I know. I'm working on an idea."

"What?" she asked eagerly.

"I'm not ready to talk about it, but I'll tell you when I can. Now, you go serve up that lunch, and I'll be right in, okay?"

Sarah smiled and gently kissed her husband's cheek.

* * * * *

For the next day or so, nothing was said about Austin or the idea Charles was working on, but finally he told her he'd like to talk. They sat down at the kitchen table with a cup of coffee, and Charles began by saying, "I wonder if the two of us and perhaps Sophie could combine forces and learn something about that afternoon."

"What do you have in mind?"

"I want to interview every nursing home resident and nurse who was at the concert that afternoon."

"The police didn't do that?"

"No, the staff swiftly got everyone back to their rooms. The cops only talked to the volunteers and guests."

"Can we just go in and do that without permission?" Sarah asked doubtfully.

"I'd like to have Hal's approval before I start, and, of course, we'll need the nursing home's permission. You can be a big help with this because you already have a relationship with the staff, and I think many of the patients would be more open with you and Sophie than with me. What do you think?"

"I think it's a great idea. Where do we start?" she asked eagerly.

"With Hal."

Charles disappeared into his den and didn't come out for nearly an hour. When he did, he didn't look particularly enthusiastic, and his lunch was now cold.

"What did he say?" Sarah asked.

"Well, he didn't forbid me to do it …" he began.

"Does he have the authority to forbid you?" Sarah asked rather indignantly.

"Yes, if he sees it as interfering with a police investigation. Fortunately, he didn't see it that way. He did say it was a waste of time because he already sent his new consultant in."

"Madison, was it?"

"Yes, Hank Madison, the retired undercover cop," Charles responded, sounding resentful.

"Did he find anything?"

"Same as when he interviewed Angela's friends—nothing."

"But he missed what could be a valuable clue when he went to Elkins. He didn't learn about Caldwell," Sarah pointed out.

"Yes, and he alienated folks while he was there, so the fact that he didn't find anything at the nursing home doesn't hold much water with me. Hal didn't say no, but he did say he wouldn't authorize it. I wasn't asking for that anyway, and I told him so. I just wanted him to be aware of what I'm doing in case the nursing home calls him."

"Good move," Sarah responded. "So where do we start and when?"

"I'm going to make an appointment with Holbrooke, the nursing home administrator, and explain my plan and tell him that you and Sophie will be involved. By the way, shouldn't you be calling Sophie to make sure she wants to be part of this?"

"You're kidding, right? Can you picture any scenario where Sophie would turn down a chance to use her 3″ by 5″ cards to solve a crime?" she asked rhetorically with a chuckle.

Charles laughed too. "I guess you're right, but tell her to keep her file cards out of sight. We don't want this to seem too official."

Charles gulped down his lunch and immediately returned to his den. Sarah headed for the attached garage, where Charles had built a cabinet for her vacuum and cleaning supplies. She had been thinking about looking for someone to do some house cleaning for her every couple of weeks but decided she wanted to continue doing it herself as long as she could. Some jobs were getting more difficult, like getting down to clean the floor and baseboards, but she had discovered that new products were coming out all the time that made those jobs more manageable.

Charles may need to build a second supply cabinet if I keep buying these gadgets, she thought as she took out her new electric floor-mopping machine. She had just started working on the kitchen floor when Charles came in and signaled for her to turn the machine off. "I have an appointment with Holbrooke right now," he announced as he pulled on his sports coat.

"I'm surprised you were able to get in so quickly," Sarah commented. "He always seems so busy."

"He had a cancellation and said if I could come right over, he could see me now."

Once she heard his car pulling out of the driveway, she turned the machine back on and continued cleaning the floor. Suddenly she remembered she hadn't told Sophie about Charles' plan. She picked up the phone to place the call but hung up without dialing, deciding instead to wait until Charles returned with Holbrooke's reaction. *No sense in setting her up for disappointment if the administrator refuses to let us in*, she told herself.

An hour later she heard Charles' car pull into the garage. "Don't forget to close the door to that cabinet," he said as he came into the kitchen, closing the garage door behind him. "I almost knocked it off its hinges when I pulled in."

"Sorry," she responded cheerfully. "Do you have good news?"

"I do. Holbrooke said it would be fine, but he wants it to be more formal than I had hoped. He gave us a small office to use and a list of staff. He wants us to make appointments with the staff and give him a copy of the schedule."

"What about the residents?"

"He said we could do a wing at a time, and to make the arrangements directly with the head nurse ahead of time."

"Okay. We can do that," she agreed.

"And he wants a list of our questions," he added with a grimace.

"That's possible, I suppose," she responded.

"It doesn't allow for following the conversation wherever it might lead," he replied with the voice of a trained investigator.

"Why don't you just add that stipulation to your list of questions? Say something at the end like, 'In some cases, it may be necessary to ask the interviewee to elaborate on their answers.'"

"Wow," he exclaimed. "I sure needed you when I did this for a living. You just got around old Holbrooke in the wink of an eye. Thanks."

"So how do you see us doing this? All three squeezed into the room at once?"

"No, I think we'll go over our questions together and then split up. I figure I'll be using the office and talking to most of the staff, and you gals will visit the patients in their rooms."

"That'll work. I'm going to go tell Sophie," Sarah said as she wrapped the cord around the handle of her electric mop.

"Go on," Charles said as he reached for the mop. "I'll put this away for you."

"Oh, you're such a sweetheart, Charles," she gushed, "but on your way to the garage, would you stop by the guest bathroom and run the mop over the floor?"

"That's not exactly on my way to the garage," he responded with a fake look of irritation as he glanced at the garage door a few feet away, "but I can do that for you."

"For us," she corrected with a sly smile.

"For us," he agreed and tossed her his car keys. "Would you fill up the tank on your way to Sophie's?"

"The gas station is not exactly on the way to Sophie's," she refuted with a frown. "In fact, it's outside the gates and a half-mile up the road."

"Precisely," he replied with a chuckle as he headed toward the hallway leading to the guest bath.

"I'll do it," she agreed, "but only because I want you to have plenty of gas when you take me out to a very expensive dinner tonight."

"Touché," he called to her from the hallway.

Chapter 16

"Okay, you and Sophie have your guide sheet, and today you have permission to visit folks on the first floor, Wing 1. Do you know your way around?"

"We're fine, Charles," Sarah replied, "but how about you?"

"I'll need a quick tour," he responded. "My cubbyhole is in the middle here by the administrative offices. I'll show you where I'll be." Sarah and Sophie followed him across the lobby and toward the line of offices.

"This is the room they gave me," he said as he opened the door to what appeared to be a large closet. There was a small desk and two chairs. He turned on the light and stepped in, but Sarah and Sophie waited in the hall, not wanting to crowd him. "Now where is your wing located?"

"Wing 1 is on this floor, right over there," Sarah said, pointing to the left. The offices and pharmacy were in the center of the medical complex with four wings extending in the shape of an X. "There are fourteen rooms on that wing." Sarah began walking toward Wing 1, and the others followed.

"So, Charles," she said, standing at the intersection of Wings 1 and 2, "there are fourteen rooms this way and another fourteen that way. Then on the opposite side of the administrative area, this design is repeated for Wings 3 and 4."

"Got it. So, let's see, there are only fourteen times four …" he muttered, doing a quick calculation in his head. "Fifty-six rooms?"

"On this floor, yes," Sarah answered. "And the design is repeated on the second floor, but two of the wings on that floor are partitioned off for memory care. Very few of those patients were attending the concert, according to the nurse I spoke with that evening."

"Okay, I've got it," Charles said. "My first appointment is scheduled in five minutes, so I'll get back to my broom closet. Call my cell if you need me. I'll meet you two at noon in the snack bar, okay?"

"We'll be there," Sophie responded, "but how many people should we talk to? Everyone in Wing 1?"

"Let the conversations determine how much time you spend. If you don't finish the wing, that's fine. Just do what you can, and hopefully something will come out of this."

"I'm nervous," Sophie admitted as she and Sarah headed toward Wing 1.

"Our friend Nadine is in Wing 1. We'll start with her, and that will help you get over your jitters."

"Great!" Sophie exclaimed enthusiastically. "But what could she have seen? She was sitting with you and me."

"It can't hurt to ask, but mostly we're visiting her because she'll be a good place to start."

No patients, Nadine included, were aware that Sarah and Sophie were coming by. "Sophie!" Nadine exclaimed when the two friends tapped on her door. "What a surprise!"

Sarah explained why they were there, and the interview ended up being an old home week for Sophie and Nadine, who immediately began talking about the concert twelve years ago. In the end, Nadine admitted that she hadn't seen anything, but she did remind Sarah about the man who tried to leave but was turned back by the policeman who was guarding the front exit.

"I'll make a note of that," Sarah said, "but supposedly everyone at the concert who wasn't a resident was questioned by the police that evening." Twenty minutes later they said their goodbyes and moved on to the first person on their new list. Nadine had looked at the list of Wing 1 residents and checked off all the ones who were at the concert. Sarah and Sophie agreed to limit their visits to those folks.

"What about the nurses?" Sophie asked.

"Charles didn't mention them, but I assume they're on his list of staff interviews."

By 11:30, they had spoken with all the people who were actually at the concert. No one remembered seeing anything except an elderly gentleman whom Sarah had noticed sitting in the front row near the hallway that led to the restrooms. "I saw a couple of women come out of the men's bathroom," he told Sarah. "I thought that was pretty strange. They'd already told us not to use the bathrooms on that floor since they'd been set aside for the performers, but this one woman didn't look like no performer."

Sarah wrote down every detail the man could remember, but he couldn't give much of a description. "A large woman," he had said. "You know, what we used to call stacked, but I don't think we're supposed to say that anymore. It's hard to keep up with all the rules, but she was good looking for sure."

"Full-figured?" Sophie asked.

"Oh yeah," he commented with a sparkle in his eye. "I like 'em robust."

"How old would you say she was?" Sarah asked.

"Oh, I can't do that anymore. Since I turned ninety, everyone looks like a kid to me."

"Are you saying she was young?" Sophie questioned.

"No, I guess I'd have to say maybe middle aged. Really, I don't have any idea about age. I just know she'd be a good handful." Dropping his head, he added, "I guess I'm not supposed to say that either."

"What about the other woman?" Sophie asked.

"What other woman?"

"You said you saw a couple of women …"

"Oh. Yeah, I think there was another one, but I didn't pay no attention." The two women spent another fifteen minutes attempting to get a description of the second woman, but the most he could remember was that there had been nothing about her that got his attention.

They thanked Mr. McGregor and asked if they could come back if they had any other questions.

"You can come visit me anytime, cutie," he said to Sophie with a wink.

Sarah chuckled to herself, realizing that her well-rounded friend was precisely the kind of woman that made Mr. McGregor's eyes twinkle.

As they were leaving the room, he called to them and said, "I just remembered that the other little lady was a nurse." They both hurried back into the room in hopes that he remembered more, but that was it. "Just some little nurse," he repeated.

Sophie, Sarah, and Charles compared notes while eating turkey sandwiches and potato chips. Sophie washed hers down with a chocolate milkshake.

Charles decided he would go back and talk to Mr. McGregor "man to man" in order to get a more specific description. "I think there were things he didn't want to say to a lady," Charles suggested. "And I'll try to track down which nurses might have been in that hallway."

As for his own interviews, one was very promising, and he planned to head over to the police department with this new information. "I had just finished interviewing the first-floor nursing staff, at least the ones on duty this morning, when a Bruce Twittle stopped by to see me. He'd heard what was going on and he wanted to tell me something he had noticed that evening."

"Had he told the police about it?" Sarah asked before he had a chance to give the details.

"No one attempted to interview the kitchen staff," he told me.

"Why would that be?" Sophie asked indignantly.

"Probably because the kitchen is on the other side of the building," Charles suggested, "but that's no excuse. Anyway," he continued, "Twittle said that sometime during the early evening a man slipped through the kitchen and out the back door."

"That's significant!" Sarah squealed, causing the woman behind the counter to jerk around to see what was happening. "Sorry," Sarah said, giving her a dismissive wave. "Did he describe the man?"

"Yeah, and maybe the department can get more detail out of him, but the guy was young, bearded, long hair in a ponytail, casually dressed—the typical person you'd see at a concert."

"But not this concert," Sarah objected. "This wasn't advertised and was only attended by residents and a very select group of invitees."

"Maybe he's one of the roadies connected with Austin?" Sophie suggested.

"That's possible. I'll turn the whole thing over to Hal. Twittle didn't seem particularly eager to talk to the police, but he said, 'Do what you have to do' when I told him I'd be relaying the information."

As they were getting into Charles' car later, he remarked, "This has been a pretty successful day, I'd say."

"I agree," Sophie replied. "We just might get my friend Austin off the hook yet."

Charles gave his wife's hand a gentle squeeze before he started the car. "We just might," he said, winking at Sarah.

* * * * *

The rest of the week wasn't as successful as that first day, although Sophie managed to have some fun. On Friday, Sarah was on her second cup of tea when Sophie rushed into the snack bar. "Boy, have I been having a great time," she announced breathlessly as she pulled out the chair opposite Sarah and called her drink order out to Bonnie, the snack bar manager. She and Sarah had decided to split up and do their interviews separately, doubling up only when they felt the need for two sets of eyes and ears.

"And how have you managed to have such a good time?" Sarah asked. "I'm finding it pretty difficult to keep asking the same questions and wading through the answers, which tend to be about everything other than the concert."

"I know," Sophie agreed. "These folks are starved for someone to talk to. I just might go back to volunteering over here ... but that's a different story. Let me tell you about my morning."

"Okay, but let's order lunch first. I'm starved."

Once they had placed their orders and settled in, Sophie announced excitedly, "I've been 'dancing with rainbows,' 'rowing a boat,' and 'parting a wild horse's mane.'"

"What are you talking about, Sophie?" Sarah asked with a frown, fearing that her friend had gone off the deep end.

"Tai chi," Sophie responded. "I passed by the activities room on my way to meet you here, and I saw this group of old folks in wheelchairs doing these very slow exercises—not even exercises," she corrected herself. "More like slow movements, and all the movements had names. The instructor invited me to join them."

"Tai chi," Sarah repeated. "I've heard of it, but I thought you did it standing. They were seated?"

"Yes, in wheelchairs, and we didn't have any trouble following the instructor."

"Wait a minute. 'We?'" Sarah interrupted. "You were doing it too?"

"Yes, I was doing tai chi."

"In a wheelchair?"

"Don't be silly. The instructor brought me a stool, and I did just great. Well, except for when I fell off the stool," she added, looking embarrassed. "That was somewhat humiliating."

"You fell? Did you hurt yourself?"

"No, but I can't speak for the man in the wheelchair behind me. I landed in his lap."

"What a terrible experience," Sarah replied sympathetically.

"Oh no, except for that little blip it was fantastic. The movements are very relaxing, and I was able to do them all. You should have seen me 'grasp the bird's tail.' Granted, I didn't do too well with the 'snake creeping through the grass,' but that's a hard one to do sitting down. Anyway, I think I'm going to find out if there's a class at the center."

"There is, but it's not seated," Sarah responded.

"Well, I'll see to it that seated tai chi is added to their program," Sophie declared. "There are plenty of people in this community with arthritis and other physical problems who aren't in the nursing home. They should be offering this to everyone. It's really great."

Bonnie served their lunch, and the two friends continued to talk about their experiences that morning.

"I didn't get anything helpful," Sarah said. "My wing must have arrived at the concert last because everyone was sitting in the back."

"Where's Charles?" Sophie asked, suddenly realizing he was missing.

"He caught Hal on a good day, I guess. Charles called him when he first got to the snack bar, and Hal suggested they meet for lunch. Charles wanted to take advantage of the opportunity to meet with him in an informal setting and perhaps learn something about the investigation."

"Did Charles learn anything new in his interviews this morning?"

"Same as you and me. Nada," Sarah replied.

"Nada? Oh," Sophie squealed. "I forgot about your Spanish lessons. How's that going?"

"I've been playing the tapes whenever I get a chance, and I'm not doing much better than I did when I was attempting to learn French. I don't think my brain is wired for foreign languages. At this point, I figure I'm lucky to have learned English."

"Why were you doing this in the first place?" Sophie asked. "You aren't planning a trip you haven't told me about, are you?"

"No, I read an article about how learning something entirely new can stimulate your brain and help maintain brain cells as you're aging."

"Like me learning to quilt?" Sophie asked eagerly.

"Exactly. And that's why I keep trying to learn a language because it clearly makes my brain work extra hard. I'll keep at it," Sarah added as she finished off her sandwich. "So, Sophie, tell me about your visits. Did anyone have any good information for us?"

"Well, there was one thing, but I doubt that it means much," Sophie said as she signaled for Bonnie to refill their drinks and asked her to bring a piece of apple pie. Sarah waited for her to continue, but Sophie seemed to be totally distracted by the pie that had been quickly placed in front of her.

"The one thing?" Sarah reminded her friend.

"Oh—remember that guy we saw trying to leave, but the cop sent him back to his seat?"

"Yeah, he was sitting in the second or third row right behind us. What about him?"

"Well, one of the women I talked to this morning said she was sitting right next to him, and that he was on his cell phone most of the time."

"That's not very helpful. Most people seem to be on their cell phones most of the time these days."

"True, but she said he was very angry when the cop wouldn't let him leave. She said he fidgeted around for a while and then got up again and headed for the ramp to the second floor with his cell phone on his ear. She said he never came back, so she figured he found another way out."

"Did she say what he looked like?" Sarah asked.

"She didn't remember much. Just that he was well dressed."

"Yes, I remember that about him," Sarah said. "He was wearing a blue suit, but I didn't see his face. I was distracted by what was going on behind the curtain. I'll remind Charles about him and tell him what you learned today. He should have Hal follow up with this woman. She might have enough of a description to help them identify the guy."

Sarah drove Sophie home, and as her friend was getting out of the car, Sarah asked if she'd like to go to dinner with her and Charles that evening. "Maybe even invite Norman?" she added.

Sophie blushed, much to Sarah's surprise. "Norman and I have a date tonight," she said, looking away.

"This sounds special," Sarah teased.

"It is," her friend responded, still avoiding Sarah's eye. "Very special."

Chapter 17

"Sarah, could you come over and help me with the 3″ by 5″ card files? I'm totally confused about our suspects."

"I'll be there just as soon as I get the breakfast dishes in the dishwasher. In the meantime, tell me about your special evening the other night. I didn't get a chance to call over the weekend to hear about it."

"You wouldn't have found me at home," Sophie admitted, glad that she was on the phone and Sarah couldn't see her face.

"Where were you?"

"Still on my date."

"Oh?" Sarah responded with an insinuation tucked into her tone.

"No, it's not what you think. You know me and my old-timey values."

"Times have sure changed," Sarah said with a sigh.

"Not for me. Anyway, Norman had a surprise for me. He took me to Chicago, and we saw the stage play *Sea Bound*. Norman knew the play took place on a quilting cruise and he knew I'd like it."

"That was Friday night?"

"We left here on Friday and we checked into the Ambassador—separate rooms, I'll have you know," she added defiantly. "Of course, they connected, but that just made it nice for visiting back and forth. We had a light dinner in the lounge that night, and then took a guided bus tour of the city the next day. We saw the play that night and took our time coming home yesterday. It was a spectacular weekend," she said wistfully.

"You don't sound totally happy about it, Sophie. Is everything okay?"

"It is, I'm just worried ..."

"About?"

"I know he's more serious about this relationship than I am. He's hinted again about making it more permanent ..."

"Marriage?"

"He hasn't said those words again, but he talks about his future like he expects me to be in it."

"And you don't want that?"

"I don't think so, Sarah. I'm happy with my life just the way it is. At least I think I am ..."

"Well, he's not asking you to make changes right now. Just enjoy what you have."

"I am getting better at that. Anyway, are you coming over?" Sophie asked, changing the subject abruptly as she often did when the conversation became too intense.

"I'll be there in ten minutes," Sarah replied.

Sarah wiped the countertops and was putting away their placemats just as Charles was heading toward the door to the garage. "What are you up to?" she asked, seeing him with an armload of tools.

"I just fixed that drip in the shower. It kept me awake again last night. How about you?"

"I'm on my way to Sophie's. The card project has gotten away from her, and she said she's feeling confused by all the potential killers floating around in her head. We're going to organize her notes. Putting everything we know on paper helps both of us see things more clearly. I'll probably be home around lunchtime."

"Actually, I probably won't. Hal called and wants me to come talk with him again. It sounds like he needs to do the same thing you and Sophie are planning to do. He said he needs to get some perspective and found our lunchtime talk the other day very helpful."

"There's a benefit to this, you know," Sarah explained. "While he's talking, he just might end up sharing some information that we don't know."

"Good thought," Charles responded as they both headed out the door. "I'll drop you off at Sophie's," he offered, and she accepted.

After having coffee and cranberry muffins fresh out of the oven, Sarah and Sophie pulled out the 3″ by 5″ box and a pad of paper. "Let's start by listing every person we've identified as a potential suspect. They're all starting to run together," Sophie said.

"Okay," Sarah started, snapping her pen open. "Let's start from the beginning. First would be Austin Bailey," she said as she wrote his name down.

"What!" Sophie screeched. "He's the one we're trying to prove *did not* do it. He doesn't belong on our list of suspects."

"Sophie, we have to be realistic and put everyone on this list who could possibly have done it. Austin belongs on our list. Just because we believe that he is innocent doesn't make it true."

"Are you on Austin's side or not?" Sophie demanded.

"I'm on Angela Padilla's side," Sarah responded. "Aren't you?"

Sophie sat quietly for a moment and then said, "Okay. I get it. Put his name down, but he didn't do it."

"Neither did most of the people on our list, but perhaps one of them did."

Sophie sighed. "Okay, put that Caldwell guy down too. You know, the guy she was dating back in Elkins who came to Middletown a few times. Do we even know the department's position on him?"

"I'm hoping Charles will find out about that today. He's doing some brainstorming with Hal just like we're doing."

"Are we brainstorming?" Sophie asked with a twinkle in her eye. It always amazed Sarah how quickly Sophie could move from one mood to another. Once Sarah had asked her friend how she was able to set anger aside so easily, and she had said, "Nothing sticks to me."

"Do you remember Caldwell's first name?" she asked Sophie.

"No need to remember," she noted proudly and grabbed her 3″ by 5″ cards. "Here it is. His name is Nathan. Nathan Caldwell. Do you want his address?"

"No, this is just a list of suspects."

"Except for Austin," Sophie muttered.

"Who else do we have?"

"The man in the suit who tried to leave the cafeteria and then vanished. Let's call him 'blue suit man,' and he needs a card."

"Okay," Sarah responded as she wrote *blue suit man* on the list. "And 'back door scruffy man,'" she added. "The guy who snuck out through the kitchen."

"Yes, I hope Charles learns where that guy stands with the department. Of course, we don't actually know who he is, so they might not have been able to question him."

"Twittle had a pretty good description. They might be able to find the guy if he was one of the roadies with Austin."

"Twittle?"

"Bruce Twittle, the kitchen worker that saw the guy leave through the kitchen," Sarah replied.

"I don't have a card on him. That was the day Charles said not to bring my cards. From now on they go everywhere I go. These cards need to be updated on the spot," Sophie grumbled.

"He needs a card, but he's not a suspect. He's just a source. So far I just have Nathan Caldwell, blue suit man, and back door scruffy man. How about the voluptuous woman exiting the men's room?"

"I have a card on her," Sophie said, thumbing through her cards. "I called her 'buxom bathroom lady,' but I changed it to 'buxom dressing room lady.' And, of course, we have 'dressing room nurse.'"

"I wish we had names for these people," Sarah commented. "Maybe Charles will come home with better information."

"We sure don't have much," Sophie concluded as she looked at the five cards in front of her. Sarah noticed with a smile that Sophie had not made a card for Austin.

"Maybe our visits to the nursing home will uncover more information. All we can do is try. In the meantime, I'm going to call Charles and ask him to stop by here when he's finished with Hal. That way, maybe we can get more information for our cards."

"Our cards?" Sophie responded indignantly. "And just when did they become *our* cards?"

"Sorry, Sophie. Your cards, of course."

Sarah hit her speed dial, and Charles answered right away. He agreed to stop at Sophie's on his way home and said it would be in about an hour or so. He also said that they would be pleased with what he had learned. Sarah heard some protesting in the background and asked what was going on.

"Hold on," Charles responded. Then she heard him say, "Hal, of course I understand that what you told me is confidential." Returning to the phone, he said to Sarah, "See you soon."

"He's learned something," Sarah said, "but whether he's going to share it with us is up in the air at the moment." She went on to tell Sophie about the sidebar conversation between Charles and Hal.

"We carry more weight than Hal," Sophie claimed. "We'll get it out of him. Let's look at that crooked table runner of mine while we wait. I did exactly what you told me to do, and now it's bowed in the opposite direction. I'm about ready to put it in the ragbag."

"Patience, Sophie. We'll fix it," Sarah replied, and they headed back to Sophie's sewing room.

* * * * *

Sarah and Charles were sitting in Sophie's living room later that afternoon, sipping wine and nibbling on cheese and crackers. The conversation had been light until Sophie finally said, "We want to know what Detective Hal told you not to tell us. No excuses, no sidestepping the issue. Just get right to it and tell us this big secret."

"There's really no big secret," Charles began, but Sophie cut him off immediately.

"Don't give us that, Charles. Tell us everything." Sophie looked at Sarah and added, "He's your husband. Demand that he talk."

Sarah laughed and said, "Well, he's not going to break a confidence just because I tell him too, but," she added, turning to Charles, "we're really all in this together. You know you can trust us with whatever you know. All we want to do is get Austin off the hook with the department. We wish we could come up with the killer, but Sophie and I would be happy just to have Austin cleared."

"All that's true," Sophie interjected. "However, as I see it, coming up with the real killer is the only sure way to clear Austin. So, Charles, please talk to us."

Charles sighed and reached for the wine bottle. "Anyone else want a refill?"

"We're fine," Sarah replied, speaking for Sophie as well. "Let's just get down to business. What have you learned?"

"Okay," Charles said reluctantly. "They tracked down the identity of the guy escaping out the kitchen door. He was, in fact, a roadie who's been traveling with Austin for the past couple of months."

"What exactly is a roadie?" Sarah asked.

"He sets up and takes down the equipment," Charles explained. "Generally, he travels with the band and maintains the equipment. The other guys in the band didn't know anything about him. They said Austin hired him and the guy kept to himself."

"And what did the department learn when they questioned the guy?" Sophie asked.

"Nothing. The guy vanished."

"Well, that's pretty telling," Sophie responded. "He sure looks guilty to me."

"And that's exactly why Austin looks guilty to the department," Charles countered. "Disappearing is not a wise move for an innocent person."

"What else did you learn?" Sophie asked, ignoring Charles' implication. "Did Hal tell you what they found out about the Caldwell guy?"

"Hank Madison, the contract ex-undercover guy, went to Elkins and reviewed the guy's record. Mostly minor offenses with the exception of a stalking charge five years ago that was dismissed but resulted in several restraining orders being issued."

"The previous girlfriend?" asked Sarah.

"Actually two different women."

"Did he question the guy?"

"Madison did, and he doesn't think the guy had anything to do with Angela's death. In fact, Caldwell had a very strong alibi for the day she was killed."

"What was it?"

"His company had sent him to a computer class in St. Louis. Madison checked it out, and the guy was not only there but did a presentation midday and was there for the second day as well."

"Couldn't he have come here and killed her and returned?" Sophie asked.

"I think it's very unlikely."

"Okay, what else?"

"They've talked to the two nursing home residents we gave them. The lady leaving the men's room turned out to be from wardrobe and was helping Angela dress. They talked to her and saw no red flags. That was actually a half hour or so before she died."

"She could have been the one who gave Angela the poison," Sophie exclaimed excitedly.

"The woman was cleared, Sophie. They know about her, and they have no reason to suspect her."

"Okay," Sophie responded as she made a note on the woman's card and asked, "Do you have her name so I can update my card?"

"It's Gloria Sutter."

"Thank you," Sophie said solemnly. It clearly pained her to dismiss the woman as a suspect. Instead, she put a question mark on the card.

"Oh, here's something I'm missing. What is the roadie's name?"

"Hawk is what they all knew him as. Austin's manager said his check was made out to John Hawkins and mailed to a bank in Texas. They're following up on that."

"So this Hawk guy is becoming a person of interest?" Sophie asked.

"He is."

"Anything else?" Sarah asked rather casually, but she suddenly became attentive when she realized Charles was hesitating. "Charles?"

"There is one other thing. It came in from Elkins, where Austin's ex-wife is living."

"She knows something?" Sarah asked curiously.

"It didn't come from her. It came from the local police department over there."

"What is it, Charles?" Sarah probed, becoming impatient.

"Before the divorce, there were several domestic violence reports made by Austin Bailey's neighbors."

Chapter 18

"I was so stunned when Charles told us about the police reports yesterday, I didn't know what to say. I don't think I slept all night." Sophie and Sarah had just arrived on the second floor of the nursing home, ready to begin their rounds in the Memory Care Unit. "Can we sit down over there before we go in?" Sophie asked. "I really need to talk with you about this. That gentle boy?"

"Sophie, I think you and I both have to face reality when it comes to Austin Bailey. First of all, he's not a boy. He's a grown man in his late thirties. And he writes incredibly beautiful songs that bring tears to our eyes. But what we aren't looking at is that we don't really know a thing about Austin Bailey, the man. Who is he? Is he as gentle as his songs, or does he have a side we'd never expect?"

"But …"

"Hear me out, Sophie. Someone who cared for him was found dead in his dressing room. There's a history of violence in his marriage. He's a prime suspect in a murder, yet he has chosen to leave town."

"So did roadie boy …"

"We aren't talking about him right now; we're talking about Austin, and I'm saying to you that we must be more realistic and open to the possibility...."

"No! I refuse to be open to any possibility, and I don't even want to hear another word about it," Sophie said as she covered both ears with her hands. "Just stop!"

Sarah sighed. *Actually,* she told herself, *it doesn't really matter whether Sophie accepts the possibility. It is what it is, and we'll just have to wait and see how it plays out. In the meantime, we have work to do.* "Come on, Sophie. Let's see if there's anyone in the Memory Care Unit who was at the concert."

Sophie stood and walked toward the door and stepped to the side as Sarah rang the bell. "I'm sorry, Sarah," she said contritely.

"I know," Sarah responded softly.

As the nurse opened the door to let them into the secure wing, someone called, "Wait for me!" They turned and saw Peggy stepping off the elevator and waving her arm.

"Peggy?" Sophie and Sarah said in unison.

"What are you doing here?" Sophie asked as Sarah stepped back into the hallway to greet their friend.

"Will you ladies please come on in so I can close the door?" the nurse requested as patiently as she could. "Three resident call lights are blinking, and I'm here by myself right now."

"Oh, sorry," Sarah said as she led Peggy and Sophie through the doorway and over to a nearby seating area. "Let's sit down for a minute and get caught up on what's happening. Peggy?"

Peggy laughed. "I know you're surprised to see me here, but I'm just as surprised to run into you two. I was going to call you this afternoon."

"So what's going on?"

"If you have time, I'll start from the beginning." Sarah and Sophie eagerly assured her they had the time, and Peggy continued. "Well, to begin with, I called the Alzheimer's folks like you recommended, and I went to several support group meetings, and everyone was saying the same thing."

"And that was?" Sophie asked.

"The same thing Charles said when he attempted to take him to the dog park," Peggy recounted. "That Leon needed to be in a safe place with people trained to care for him. I wasn't ready to hear that, so, with the Alzheimer's Association's help I was able to find a male home health aide who could come help me with him. They sent me this nice young man named Brian. He helped me get Leon up and dressed every day, and for a few days Brian was even able to get Leon to take his medications."

"That must have made life easier for you," Sarah said.

"And safer," Sophie added.

"Yes, for a few days. I thought it was going to work out, but last week it all fell apart."

"What happened?" Sophie asked.

"Leon got violent with both of us. He knocked Brian down and broke his wrist and then he came after me. He was totally out of control and didn't seem to know who I was," she added despairingly. "Brian pulled me into the bedroom and locked the door. He called the police. I was pleading with him not to, but in my heart I knew it had to be done."

"What did the police do when they got there?" Sophie asked.

"They brought Leon back in. They said he was out in the middle of the street half-dressed and yelling obscenities. They sent for an ambulance and took him right to the hospital. His doctor met us there and sedated him and ran some tests. They finally got him under control, and the doctor talked to me about keeping him a few days for more tests and getting him properly medicated. Again, I had hope that he could come home and I could care for him, but it didn't work out that way."

"What happened?" Sophie asked again.

"The doctor said there was no way either of us would be safe at home. He recommended that Leon be admitted to a nursing home when he left the hospital. I guess I knew it would come to that, but I kept hoping ..."

"That's perfectly normal, Peggy. We all hope for the best, but sometimes the best thing isn't what we thought it was. I think you and Leon are both better off now."

"Actually, Sarah," Peggy said, laying her hand gently on Sarah's arm, "you're absolutely right. I'm ashamed to say this, but I feel safe for the first time in several years. Even Leon seems more at ease. Of course, he's loaded with medication," she added, looking contrite, "but the doctor told me that he'll pass through this stage and life will become easier for him and for those of us around him."

"Yes, it's a progressive disease, and there seem to be stages," Sophie interjected. "My husband went through that combative stage but he was already in the nursing home, and it wasn't nearly as bad as it was for you, and after a while he became calmer. Of course, he didn't know where he was, but he didn't seem to care. He got to a point where he seemed pleased to see me when I visited, although he clearly had no idea who I was."

"That must have been hard for you," Peggy responded. "Recognition comes and goes with Leon. At least for now."

"Are you okay with all this?" Sophie asked, remembering how hard it had been for her.

"It's a big relief, Sophie. I've been so afraid he'd wander off and something would happen to him."

"And honestly, Peggy," Sarah said, "I was afraid for you."

"I'll have to admit that I was frightened too. Leon wasn't the man I married. Like I told you, he was always hard-headed and wanted things his way, but the past year … well, I'm just glad it's done. I go to my support meetings, and I visit him every day, sometimes twice. But sometimes I can't help but wonder …"

"You've done the right thing, Peggy," Sarah said reassuringly.

"I know, and I have you two to thank. There's no telling what would have happened if we'd continued like we were."

"So," Sophie said, ready to change the subject, "does this mean you're coming back to the quilt club?"

"It sure does."

"This week?"

"Yes," Peggy said, laughing. "I've really missed the group."

The three women sat for another few minutes, catching Peggy up on the placemat project and the plans for the upcoming meeting. Finally, Peggy stood and said, "Okay, I'm off to see my bear. Take care, friends, and I'll see you Tuesday night."

They watched to see what room she went into and agreed to skip that room. "I don't want to upset him," Sarah explained, and Sophie agreed. They headed for the nurses' station just as two nurses were coming on duty.

"Lucia, could you help these ladies? They want to talk with anyone who went down to the Austin Bailey concert. You were here that day, right?" the head nurse asked.

"I was," Lucia replied, "but Mr. Holland was the only one from this wing that I took down. Do you want to see him? I'm not sure how much talking he'll do. He has a strange way of communicating."

"How's that?" Sophie asked.

"He carries his cell phone everywhere ..."

"Everyone communicates that way these days," Sophie replied.

"No, he's not talking on the phone. He's taking pictures. Thousands of them! He just shows you a picture of whatever he wants."

"Do you think he took pictures at the concert?"

"The concert that never was?" Lucia asked rhetorically. "We were all so disappointed. And that girl! She was such a sweet thing. I just can't believe ..." and Lucia went on ruminating about the tragedy.

"Did he take pictures while he was downstairs?" Sarah repeated.

"Sure, he takes pictures everywhere."

They had arrived at Mr. Holland's room, and there was a flash of light as the patient took their pictures, five or six in succession. Sarah and Sophie introduced themselves, and he took another picture. They asked his permission to sit down and visit with him, and he took another picture. And then another once they were seated.

Their attempts at conversation were met by silence and indifference until Sarah said, "I'd love to see your pictures." Mr. Holland dropped the cell phone into the pocket of his pajama top and grumbled. The women continued to search for a subject that might interest the man, but their attempts were ignored, and the man ultimately fell asleep in his chair.

As the two women left the room, Sophie said, "We have to get ahold of that camera."

"I know."

"I'm going to go back and slip it out of his pocket while he's asleep," Sophie said, turning to return to the room.

"No, Sophie," Sarah insisted. "We can't do that, but perhaps Hal can. Let's go home."

* * * * *

Sarah had no sooner walked in the front door when she got a call from Vicky, the volunteer coordinator at the nursing home. "Vicky, what a surprise! It's been a long time since we talked."

"I have a strange message to deliver," Vicky began. "I got a call from the nurses' station in Wing 2 of the Memory Care Unit where you were visiting today. It seems they have a patient who is insisting on seeing you."

"What? Mr. Holland?"

"Yes, that's his name."

"But he wouldn't talk to us at all and finally just turned and went to sleep during our visit. He said he wants to see us?"

"Well, he wants to see you. He showed your picture to the nurse and motioned that you should come to see him."

"This is so strange," Sarah responded, "but I'm glad. I'll be right over."

Sarah debated whether to call Sophie but decided to honor the man's request and go alone. He had many pictures of Sophie but had chosen to show only hers to the nurse.

When she arrived back at the nursing home, it was approaching lunchtime, and the meal cart was sitting outside Mr. Holland's room. When he saw her, he motioned for her to come in and sit down. At that moment, an aide brought his lunch in and placed it on the tray next to his chair. He glanced at the food and, looking annoyed, waited for the woman to leave the room. He then reached into the pocket of his robe and pulled out a tattered picture, which had clearly been handled often over the years. He handed the picture to Sarah.

Sarah looked at it and squinted her eyes to see it more clearly. *What's this?* She reached into her purse for her reading glasses and looked again. Although not an exact image by any means, the woman in the picture reminded Sarah of herself. The hair was the same color and similarly styled, but it was the eyes in particular that caught her attention. Though the woman in the picture was younger than Sarah, the similarity was striking.

"Who is this?" Sarah asked, and the man placed both hands on his heart.

"Your wife?"

Tears welled up in his eyes. "I'm so sorry," Sarah replied and moved her chair closer. "I remind you of her?"

He attempted to wipe the tears away before they began to fall. The two sat quietly for a long time, each lost in thought. She'd experienced this herself, particularly in the years just following her husband's death. She'd see a man with similar features and the grief would wash over her again, sometimes nearly taking her breath away.

Slowly the man reached inside his robe and pulled the cell phone out of his pajama pocket. He turned it on and handed it to Sarah. She wasn't sure what to do, so she just held it and looked at him until he pointed to the camera and to her.

"You want me to look at the pictures?"

He nodded once. *He understands me*, she realized. She decided to explain to him what she was looking for. She wasn't sure how much he'd comprehend, but it seemed worth a try, and he apparently trusted her.

"The day of the Austin Bailey concert a young girl was murdered," she began. "I'm trying to find out what happened to her. I heard that you were taking pictures and I thought you might have one of someone perhaps acting strangely or trying to sneak out."

Mr. Holland reached for the cell phone, and Sarah's heart sank. *I was mistaken.* She watched him as he slowly thumbed through the pictures. After ten minutes or so, she was beginning to get uncomfortable from sitting on the hard chair watching him meticulously go through his pictures. She was thinking about leaving when he suddenly passed the phone to her.

She looked at the picture and gasped. It was the man in the blue suit walking up the ramp at the back of the room. Mr. Holland had obviously been seated right by the ramp.

The picture was clear, the man's face in profile. "This is wonderful," she exclaimed.

Mr. Holland reached for the camera, moved to the next picture, and passed it back to her. A full frontal picture of the man's face. She touched the screen and gently enlarged it until his features filled the frame. "Oh, Mr. Holland, you have been a tremendous help. May I send these two pictures to my phone?"

He didn't respond, but there was the faint beginning of a smile on his lips and a softness in his eyes.

There's so much more going inside your head than people realize, she said to herself as she smiled back. She quickly emailed the pictures to her own cell phone and checked to make sure they had arrived. She then asked if it was okay to look at the other pictures he took that day. He didn't object, which she assumed was passive permission.

He watched as she slowly looked at each picture. He had taken several dozen that afternoon and evening, and she sent a few of them to her own phone, although she didn't see anything significant in them. They were overviews of the room, and she thought perhaps Charles or the police might spot something useful. Most of the others were headshots of fellow patients and several of his nurse, Lucia.

As she stood to leave after thanking him profusely, she bent over and kissed his cheek. "May I come see you again?" she asked, and again she saw the faint glimmer of a smile. "I'll take that to be a yes," she said with a warm smile.

Chapter 19

"You'll never guess what I have," Sarah announced as she walked in her front door.

"And I have news for you," her husband responded with a twinkle in his eye.

"Who's going first?"

"Well, perhaps 'ladies first' is the principle we should apply. On the other hand, I know you'd love to hear ..."

"Okay, okay. Charles, you go first. It won't be as good as mine, but go ahead. What is your news?"

"Austin Bailey is back."

"Oh, Charles, you do have the best news! I'm so glad he came back. Have you talked to him? Did he say where he's been? And does Hal know?"

"That's a lot of questions for one old retired detective, but I'll take them in order. I have talked to him, and he's fine. He's been on his grandmother's farm taking care of her animals and settling the estate. He's the executor, so it's been lots of work."

"I'm sorry, Charles, but I don't understand why he just left. All he had to do was tell Hal that he needed to take care of these things. He didn't need to just run off and make himself look guilty." Sarah was clearly annoyed. "Besides, we all worried about him."

"I know, but he also told me that he needed to be alone. He was grief-stricken by the loss of Angela, and he had lost his grandmother just a few weeks before that. He said he spent his days working hard on the farm and his evenings sitting under the stars thinking, grieving, and singing. He's written a few songs that he said may be his best."

"And does Hal know he's back?" she asked.

"Yes. Austin went by the station and talked to him. He said Hal seemed cool, but he also thinks Hal understands why he left. I don't think it's changed anything. He's still a person of interest. …"

"Which means he's a suspect," Sarah interjected.

"Yes, but one of several, and personally I don't think Hal has Austin high on the list. As a matter of fact, he's very interested in finding the roadie guy that snuck out the kitchen door."

"Does he have leads? The guy just dropped out of sight, didn't he?"

"Yes, but they have developed some promising leads among the band. There's a young girl that follows the band everywhere. …"

"What we used to call a groupie?" Sarah asked.

"Yeah, I guess. Anyway, she had her eye on Austin, but she got to know this guy Hawk pretty well they say."

Sarah sat down at the kitchen table across from her husband. "I'm glad he's home. Sophie will be pleased too. I'd like to call and tell her. Is that okay?"

"Sure. It's no secret. But first, what about your news?"

"Ah," she responded mischievously. "Just take a look at what I have," and she handed him her cell phone with the man in the blue suit front and center.

"Where on God's green earth did you get this?" Charles exclaimed with astonishment. She told him the story of Mr. Holland, and he listened intently, asking a few questions. "Interesting guy," he commented as he transferred the photos to his own phone and immediately forwarded them to Hal at the police department along with a note that said, "My wife is a genius!"

"Could we invite Austin to dinner tonight?" Sarah asked when he finished talking to the detective, who had called him the moment he received the photographs.

"I don't see why not, but I think we should keep it low-key—not a lot of questions."

"Are you suggesting that I not invite Sophie?"

"I guess that's what I'm suggesting."

"I'll talk to her. She'd be brokenhearted if she knew we had him here without her."

"I'm holding you responsible," Charles teased with a playful wink. He knew that no one could control Sophie if she got it into her head to inundate the singer with questions.

When Sarah called Sophie to tell her Austin was home, she figured everyone living between them could hear Sophie's squeal. "Did he tell you where he's been and why he left right in the middle of the investigation?" Sophie asked. "And does he know how guilty that made him look? And what about all those domestic violence reports Hal discovered back in his hometown—our hometown? What does he have to say for himself?"

"Okay, Sophie. Now I want you to listen carefully. Austin is coming to dinner tonight. ..."

"I'll be there," Sophie announced, assuming an invitation was going to follow.

"Wait. Let me finish. Charles has said that we can invite Austin only if we promise not to interrogate him or make him uncomfortable. He's been back home settling his grandmother's estate and spending time alone dealing with all his emotions—he's grieving the loss of a young girl who was like a daughter to him and the grandmother who raised him. And he's a prime suspect in a murder case. It got to be more than he could deal with, and he went back home to the farm to sort out his feelings and recuperate. ..."

"And you don't want me to bombard him with questions," Sophie recited. "I understand that. May I come if I promise to behave?"

Sarah laughed. "I knew you'd understand. Come over at 7:00 for drinks, and we're going to cook steaks outside."

"I'll be there with bells on, and my mouth closed," Sophie promised—a promise she was totally unable to keep.

Fortunately, Austin was in a relaxed mood and had brought his guitar. They sat around the firepit watching the steaks sizzle while Austin serenaded them with two of his new songs.

"I had lots of time to write," Austin said. "There's something about that Missouri sky that has always inspired me."

"I love your new songs," Sarah commented. "They are very emotional pieces. They touch my heart."

"I was feeling particularly melancholy. For one insane moment, I actually thought about giving up the travel and just staying on at the farm. Grandma left it to me. I think she had the idea I might do just that."

"Don't you have a sister?" Sarah asked, but then realized it wasn't an appropriate question because what she was really asking was why he got it all. "Oh, sorry," she added.

"That's okay. My grandmother also held the deed on my father's family farm west of Elkins. They've had hired folks living out there running it for years—actually, since my father's folks died. Anyway, Grandma left that to my sister. Grandma's farm meant more to me than to Sis since I pretty much grew up there."

Everyone grew quiet as Charles turned the steaks and said, "It won't be long now."

"So, why are we ignoring the elephant in the room?" Austin asked suddenly, looking from Sophie to Sarah and back again.

"The elephant?" Sophie repeated, looking confused.

"My status as the prime suspect in a murder. The fact that I up and left town in the middle of the investigation. The fact that it really looks bad. No one has said a word about it."

"Well," Sophie began, "since you brought it up, I wanted the answers to all those questions, but Sarah explained to me why you needed to get away. And I understand, but if you're really interested in talking about it, I'd love to tell you what Sarah and I have been doing and what we've found out."

"I'd love to hear," Austin replied, reaching into the cooler for another beer.

"Well, dinner's ready right now," Charles announced, "so all that will have to wait. Come find a seat. Sarah, would you bring the salad out?" Within a few minutes, they were sitting around the picnic table, laughing, sipping wine, and devouring four very large and perfectly cooked steaks.

"What a dinner," Austin commented as Sarah took their plates away and returned with dessert and coffee. "Now, Sophie, how about catching me up on what you gals have been up to."

"What we've done is provide the police department with at least three, possibly four, suspects, and what we're hoping is that at least one of these people will take your place at the top of the list."

"And I'd like to add," Charles interjected, "that I believe that's exactly what's happening. The department is hot on the trail of one of your roadies …"

"Who?" Austin asked, looking surprised.

"John Hawkins," Charles replied.

"Hawk? Why would he kill Angie? I don't think he even knew her."

"Well, let's not argue with the police. It's a good thing they are looking at other people."

"I know, but Hawk?" Austin repeated, shaking his head. "I don't see it."

"Then there's this guy we call 'blue suit man,'" Sophie continued. "He tried to get out of the room once the police arrived and finally did manage to sneak out by going up to the second floor."

"Back to Hawk," Austin said. "What does he have to say about it? He says he's innocent, doesn't he?"

"He hasn't said anything," Charles responded. "He snuck into the kitchen and took off out the side door and hasn't been seen or heard from since. But Hal says they have a few leads. They are pursuing him."

"Hmm," Austin reacted thoughtfully. "And you said there are others?"

"Well," Sophie replied, "there's this guy, Caldwell, that Angie dated briefly back in Elkins. She stopped seeing him after a couple of dates, but her friends said he followed her here, though he denies it. He has a record in Elkins for stalking another young woman," she added.

"He also has an almost airtight alibi," Charles broke in.

"Almost?" Austin asked.

"He was speaking at a conference of some kind," Charles explained, "and he would barely have had time to make the trip, much less pull off a murder while here. Hal is sending one of his new rookies out to make the trip and see if it's within the realm of possibility."

"Oh, and there was a voluptuous woman," Sophie added, "seen leaving your dressing room at about the time of the murder. She was later identified as the wardrobe woman, but …"

"Glorious Gloria?" Austin said with a laugh. "I assure you she's no killer. Gloria keeps us all looking spiffed up like some mother hen. All she had to work with was us scruffy cowboys, and she was delighted to have a pretty young woman to dress up. No, Gloria is out."

"That's pretty much what the police said," Sophie conceded.

After a short period of thoughtful silence, Austin finally said, "Well, this is somewhat encouraging, I guess. But this Caldwell guy sounds like the only one with a motive. I really don't think Hawk ever met Angie, and your blue suit guy was probably just late for dinner."

"It's all information the police weren't collecting," Sophie asserted gruffly.

"How did you gals get all these leads anyway?" Austin asked.

Over the next few hours, Sarah and Sophie shared their many experiences while wandering the halls of the nursing home in search of anyone who might have seen something suspicious the afternoon of the concert that never happened.

"I'm sure glad you gals are on my side," Austin announced as he stood to leave.

Sophie and Sarah exchanged a look but didn't respond.

* * * * *

"I guess you noticed that I didn't bring up the police reports about domestic violence at Austin's house back when he was still married," Sophie said the next morning. She had appeared at Sarah's door a little after eight on the pretense of walking her dog. Sarah knew she rarely walked that far with Emma. Her gentleman friend, Norman, often took Emma on long walks, but Sophie usually took her out in the backyard.

"None of us brought it up," Sarah responded as she poured coffee for the two of them. "Have you had breakfast?" she asked.

"Yes," Sophie replied, "I had a bowl of cereal, but if you have something else in mind …"

"I was getting ready to stick a waffle in the toaster. Charles has gone to the gym, and I thought I'd have a waffle with peanut butter and honey. Join me?"

"Sure," Sophie agreed. She crinkled her nose slightly at the thought of frozen store-bought waffles, but once it was in front of her, she ate it with gusto and asked for seconds.

"I guess you are wondering why I'm here so early," she finally said as she attempted to wipe some spilled honey from the front of her sweatshirt with her napkin.

"Here, let me get you a wet cloth," Sarah responded, ignoring the question.

"Well, here's what I've been thinking about." Sophie licked some honey from her wrist and then used the rag to wipe honey off the table. "Messy stuff," she muttered. "I've been thinking about those reports of domestic violence, and you know that's my hometown. I still know people there. Well, I know a few old people anyway. I lived just two blocks over from where Austin and his wife lived. Of course, it wasn't at the same time. I'm at least forty years older than the boy, but I'll bet some of my old neighbors are still around."

"Where are you going with this, Sophie?" Sarah asked, sitting down across the table from her friend.

"I was thinking about asking Norman to go back to Elkins with me and see if we could find anyone who lived there when Austin and his wife were still together. That would have been about four or five years ago, and I'm sure some neighbors would talk to us."

"I don't know, Sophie. Do you mean just talk to the older people that you know?"

"Well, maybe I could talk to some of the other neighbors, too."

"I think we should talk to Charles about this," Sarah advised.

"I disagree. I once heard that if you don't think you'll like the answer, don't ask the question."

"Sophie, I don't think you should do it."

"What could happen? I just want to know if the young man I so admire is a wife beater. Is that too much to ask? And don't forget, Norman will be with me."

Sarah sighed. "I don't see how I can keep this from Charles."

"I do. I won't tell you if or when I go. That way you won't know anything to tell him."

"Sophie, I already know, and I don't like it."

"Well, just forget we talked. Do you want to get together this afternoon to do some sewing?"

Sarah sighed again.

The two women ended up making plans to sew at Sophie's house later. Sarah had left her Featherweight set up in her friend's sewing room, and their projects were ready to work on. Sarah had been making Missouri Star blocks for Austin's memory quilt and only needed a few more before she could begin putting the blocks together. "Come on over when you're ready," Sophie said as she headed for the door.

"Aren't you forgetting something?" Sarah asked.

Sophie stopped. "What? Oh, my dog!" Sarah had already opened the door to the backyard, and Emma came romping across the floor and stopped at Sophie's feet.

Over the next week, no one spoke of the contemplated trip to Elkins.

Chapter 20

B y the end of the week, Sarah had her Missouri Star quilt finished except for the final border. She suddenly realized she hadn't made arrangements with Kimberly and Christina, her long-arm quilters.

"I'm sorry, Sarah, but we just made a commitment to that new bed-and-breakfast that's opening next month. They have eight quilt tops ready to be quilted. I don't think we can take anything else for a few weeks."

Sarah was disappointed. She had hoped to give Austin the quilt soon because she felt it would bring him some degree of comfort. She asked if the sisters knew of anyone else, although she was reluctant to use another quilter.

Kimberly left the phone for a minute, and Sarah could hear her speaking with her sister. When she returned, Kimberly said, "Tell you what, Sarah. If you can get the quilt over to us first thing in the morning, we'll squeeze you in. The bed-and-breakfast isn't opening for at least a month, and they have requested a simple allover design. Those eight quilts will go very quickly."

"This one will need custom quilting," Sarah said reluctantly.

"That's fine," Kimberly agreed. "I've seen your quilt top, and we already have an idea for the quilting."

"I'll get it to you tomorrow morning," Sarah promised.

Sarah started to call Sophie to tell her the news but decided to spend her time finishing the quilt. She isolated herself in her sewing room for the next few hours and finished the quilt except for making the binding, which she decided to do that evening.

The following morning, Sarah spread the quilt top across her bed and called Charles in to see it. "That's spectacular!" he exclaimed enthusiastically. "It reminds me of the night sky you told me about when you and Sophie were in Missouri."

"Thank you, Charles. That's what I was hoping to create. Do you think Austin will like it?"

"He will," Charles replied, "but I think you should enter it in one of the shows first. This looks like a winner to me."

"I appreciate that, but I want him to have it as soon as possible. I think he needs it. It lets him know that there are people who believe in him, and it's a reminder of something he holds dear."

"What does Sophie think of it?"

"She hasn't seen it finished, but I'll call her now. Actually," Sarah muttered pretty much to herself, "Sophie might like to ride with me when I take the quilt to Kimberly." She picked up the phone and tapped Sophie's speed dial number.

"Is Sophie going with you?" Charles asked later as Sarah was preparing to leave.

"She wasn't home. I left her a message, but I need to leave. If she calls, tell her I had to go on without her, but I'll call when I get back."

"Would you like to go out to dinner tonight?" Charles asked. "You've been closed up in that room for days."

"I'd love that, Charles. Italian?"

"Comfort food it is!"

It was the following day before Sarah realized that Sophie hadn't returned her call. She hooked Barney's leash onto his collar and headed out for a walk, intending to stop by Sophie's and see if she and Emma wanted to join them. There was no answer when she tapped on the door, so she knocked harder. "Sophie? Are you in there?" Her car was in the driveway, and Sarah began to worry. She pulled out her cell phone and dialed Sophie's number.

"Hi," her friend answered in an unusually grim tone.

"Sophie, are you alright?"

"I am, but I'm extremely disappointed."

"Well, come open the door so Barney and I can come in and hear about it."

"Oh, I'm not home."

"Where are you?" Sarah sat down on Sophie's porch rocker, and Barney curled up at her feet.

Sophie didn't respond right away, but then said, "I guess I can tell you now. Norman and I are on our way back from Elkins." Sarah quickly reviewed the last few days and realized she hadn't talked to Sophie for almost a week.

"You sound terrible. Do you want to wait until you get home to tell me about it?"

"Yes, but I want to tell you one thing now. Austin Bailey is not the man we thought he was. I'm so disappointed in him. He seemed so gentle …"

"Sophie?"

"We'll be home in an hour. I'll talk to you then."

Sarah took Barney to the dog park, where he spotted one of his best friends, a black-and-white schnauzer who was about the same age and had the same energy level as Barney. He walked over to his friend, and they sniffed their hellos. Sarah sat down and watched their gentle play and remembered the days when Barney would have been running in circles around the park. *He's getting old just like the rest of us*, she reminded herself.

It was at that moment that the thought hit her. *Sophie's birthday!* Her friend hadn't had much to say about it since the day they were driving home from Elkins, and it had totally slipped Sarah's mind. *We need to have a party.*

"Come on, Barney," she called. "We have a party to plan." Barney begrudgingly followed Sarah to the gate and sat at her feet while she snapped the leash back on.

When she got home, she talked to Charles about it. He was all for the idea, but he brought up an important point. "What about Norman? He's a professional party planner. Don't you think he'd want to be involved?"

"You're right, Charles. I don't know how I missed that. He probably already has something in the works. I need to talk to him before I do anything."

At that moment, the phone rang. "Sarah, is it okay for Norman and me to stop by your house before he takes me home? We want to talk with you two about something."

"Of course, Sophie. How far away are you?"

"Only about twenty minutes," Sophie responded. "See you soon."

"You heard that, right?" Sarah asked, realizing that she had had the speaker on. "Maybe we can get Norman aside while they're here."

Unfortunately, no one was in the mood to discuss a party after Sophie delivered her depressing news.

* * * * *

Sophie and Norman had been gone for almost an hour, and Sarah and Charles were still sitting in the living room attempting to digest this new vision of the man they had grown to care deeply about.

"I find this all so hard to believe, Charles. Austin seems like such a warm and kindhearted man. I can't imagine him doing the things Sophie described."

"Sophie got it directly from the ex-wife, Sarah. It's the reason she left him; she refused to take the abuse any longer. You have to give her credit for leaving. So many women just stay, saying things like, 'He didn't mean to hurt me,' or 'He apologized,' or my all-time favorite, 'He said he'll never do it again.'"

"I sure don't feel like giving him a quilt after this. Who is this man, Charles? How could I have been so wrong?"

"How could *we* have been so wrong?" he asked. "I'm usually good at reading people, especially the ones who are trying to present themselves in a good light when they're actually bad to the core."

"Do you think he killed Angela?" Sarah asked in a voice so low Charles wasn't sure he heard her.

"Do I think he killed her? Sarah, I can't answer that. My radar is totally off on this one. I'm just glad this isn't my case to solve. If he did kill her, he almost got away with it. Thank goodness for Sophie."

"Will Hal be talking to the ex-wife?"

"He will now."

"Oh, Charles, I feel so bad about all this."

"Me too, hon … me too."

* * * * *

"Sarah, where are you? The meeting is starting, and everyone is asking about you. Aren't you coming?"

"Sorry, Sophie. Actually, I completely forgot about the quilt club meeting tonight. I've been trying to reconcile this new information about Austin with the Austin I thought I knew, and it just has me so upset."

"I know what you mean, but staying home and trying to figure it out won't help. Eventually, the police will figure out what happened, and if Austin actually did kill Angela, we'll just have to accept it."

"And you think that's a possibility?" Sarah asked.

"After talking to his ex-wife, I'll have to admit it's a possibility. Actually, from some of the things she told us, I think she's lucky to be alive herself."

"Sophie! How can you say that?"

"Sarah, you didn't hear the details, and I'm sure we only heard a small part of what he did to her. She was too ashamed to tell us much."

"Ashamed?"

"Because she knows she should have left him long before she did. I don't know what it is with these abused wives. They just keep believing that things will get better. Linda suffered twenty years of marriage and finally just couldn't take it anymore, and she left him. She went to a women's shelter, and they helped her get her life back together."

"I need to reevaluate everything I've believed about this man," Sarah stated with a note of sadness in her voice.

"I know, but like we told you last night, Norman and I spent over two hours with her, and you couldn't miss her pain. I still can't picture this side of Austin, but she knows him better than we do."

"So what's going on at the quilt club meeting tonight?" Sarah asked, wanting to change the subject.

"Christina brought your Missouri Stars quilt in, all quilted and bound. It looks incredible. She let me have a peek, but she doesn't want to show it to the group. She said that's for you to do. Won't you come on over?" Sophie pleaded. "We need you to help us plan our next group project."

Sarah sighed and decided she was making a mistake. Isolating herself and thinking about Austin wasn't going to help anyone. "Okay, I'll be there in fifteen minutes."

"Bring your scrappy quilt pattern book, would you? I want to suggest we use one of the patterns for the club project."

"What project?" Sarah asked.

"Ruth is getting ready to tell us about it. We'll wait for you."

"See you in a few," Sarah ended as she hung up and turned to Charles. "I'm going to go to the meeting after all. Sophie seems to think I should be there."

"I agree with your friend. Moping around here isn't going to help. Besides, I've invited Austin to drop by and have a beer with me tonight, and I'm not sure you're ready to see him."

"You're right. Are you going to ask him about all this?"

"I'll play it by ear. Hal is waiting for Elkins PD to forward him the domestic disturbance reports from back then, so I'll get the details either way."

Sarah grabbed a jacket and her keys and left without any projects to work on at the club meeting. She didn't feel like sewing, but thought she might like to just thumb through Ruth's books.... "Oh, the book!" she said aloud as she was getting into the car.

"You back already?" Charles teased as she rushed through the kitchen on her way to her sewing room.

"Forgot something," she called over her shoulder. When she stepped into the room, she saw the tote bag that contained her ongoing hexagon project. She decided to grab that also, just in case. As she drove toward Stitches, she was aware that she was feeling better already. *Isolating myself never helps my mood. When will I learn?*

Everyone greeted Sarah enthusiastically when she arrived. Ruth held up a note from the local women's shelter thanking the group again for the quilts they had made the previous year for the residents' beds. Ruth began reading the note aloud: " 'We were wondering if your group would be willing to make a quilt that we could raffle off this winter as a fundraiser. We'd be happy to pay in advance for the fabric and any related costs.' " Ruth glanced around the room and asked, "So, what do you think?"

The group was excited about the project and immediately began discussing ideas for the design. "Sarah brought her new scrappy quilt project book along," Sophie announced. "There's a quilt on, I think, page eighteen, that would be fun to make in a group, and it uses lots of scraps. I'm sure we could all spare some of our own scraps." Everyone chuckled in agreement.

The group passed the book around and agreed it would be an excellent choice. "It's very scrappy," Delores said, "and if we each make a dozen or so blocks, we could easily make it queen size."

Going over the pattern, everyone made notes regarding how to make the block. "What about the copyright?" someone asked.

"Not a problem," Ruth responded. "This is basically the Dutchman's Puzzle, and it's an old design from the 1800s and in the public domain. It's a simple four-patch made with eight Flying Geese." Looking at the picture in the book, she added, "We wouldn't use this quilter's unique layout. We'll come up with our own design. Does everyone know how to make the Flying Geese?"

Three members shook their heads.

"Let's have a quick lesson," Ruth began. "Delores, can you tell everyone how to do it?"

Delores had her machine set up, and she continued, "Even better—I'll make a few, and we can use them in the quilt. I have a bag of scraps right here." The group congregated around Delores as she demonstrated a quick method for making the Flying Geese blocks. Within a few minutes, she had the first block completed.

"And," Delores admonished, "don't turn your blocks in unless they are neatly pressed and measure exactly eight and a half inches!" Delores was a stickler for neatly ironed and carefully measured blocks.

"How soon should we have these done?" Allison asked.

"Let's try to finish the quilt before the holidays," Ruth suggested. "We can work on the blocks at home and at our next meeting and see how we're doing."

As they were leaving, Allison cornered Sarah and asked about Caitlyn. "She hasn't contacted me yet," the young woman complained.

"I know," Sarah responded. "Her father is saying the same thing. She's very busy with school and adjusting to a very different environment. Have you been to Los Angeles?"

"Never, but I'm hoping to go visit Caitlyn if she goes back next year."

Sophie walked up at that moment, lamenting that they had two cars and couldn't go home together. "Why don't you stop by my house?" Sarah suggested on the spur of the moment. "Austin was coming by to see Charles this evening."

"Do you think Charles would mind the intrusion?" Sophie asked.

"They've had over two hours together, and I think you and I need to see him and get that initial contact over with."

"And I want to ask him if he beat his wife."

"Sophie! You are uninvited. We can't …"

"Sarah, will you ever learn not to take me seriously?"

"I doubt it," Sarah mumbled as she walked toward her car. "See you there," she called to her friend.

Austin's car wasn't in the driveway when they arrived, but Sophie parked and followed Sarah into the house. She wanted to hear what Charles had to say about the evening. Unfortunately, she didn't learn much. Charles told them that he hadn't broached the subject, and Austin certainly hadn't.

"We drank a couple of beers and watched the game," Charles responded when Sophie asked about their evening. "Guy stuff," he added. "What did you two do this evening?"

"Gal stuff," Sophie mentioned as she walked out the door.

Chapter 21

"I've been wondering about something," Sophie began as the waitress was walking away after serving their sandwiches and drinks. Sarah and Charles had invited her to join them for a spur-of-the-moment lunch at a local pub.

"What's that?" Charles asked as he carefully removed the onions from his burger.

"We know Angela was poisoned, and we've been concentrating on who might have been responsible for it, but we've never talked about how she was poisoned. Charles, you must know."

Charles glanced away from Sophie and didn't answer right away.

"Charles?" Sarah said with a frown. "That's an excellent question. How was she poisoned?"

"Well," he began reluctantly, "the department chose to withhold that information."

"Why in the world would they want to withhold it?" Sophie inquired indignantly.

Before he had a chance to respond, Sarah added, "But you know, don't you? Are you withholding it as well?"

"Sarah, this is not unusual. In most cases, a piece of information is held back. That's so we ... well, the police ..." he clarified, since he was no longer a part of the department, "can use it in their interrogations. It becomes something that only the police and the guilty person know. They hope their suspect will slip up. ...."

"We understand that," Sophie said. "But why would you withhold it from us? Are you afraid we'll tell someone and ruin ...?"

"No, Sophie," Charles interrupted. "It's not like that at all. I spent thirty-five years as a cop and following cop rules. They just come naturally to me. It never occurred to me that I could share that information with you two, but, of course, I trust you both."

"So?"

"What?"

"Tell us now," Sophie demanded.

Charles glanced around, looking uncomfortable. He then specified, barely above a whisper, "The poison was in a Coke bottle."

"A Coke bottle?" Sophie squealed. "Was it her Coke bottle? Where did she get it? Who ...?"

"I don't know the answer to any of your questions," Charles replied. "The bottle was found by her body in the dressing room. There was enough left in the bottle for the drug to be identified by the lab."

"Lots of people were in and out of that dressing room," Sarah said softly, respecting her husband's desire to keep the information confidential. "The men's room, right?"

"Right. The men's room had been converted to a temporary dressing room."

"Austin's dressing room," Sarah clarified but with a question mark in her voice.

"Mainly, yes," Charles replied, "but Angie was in it when she died."

"And Austin wasn't," Sophie confirmed. "He'd already gone backstage, right?"

"Right."

The three sat silently for a few moments. Their sandwiches remained untouched. They were each deep in thought.

Finally, Sophie said what they were all thinking. "Maybe the poison wasn't intended for Angela."

Goosebumps crept up Sarah's spine as she realized the implications. *Could the intended victim have been Austin and not Angela at all?*

* * * * *

"What did Hal have to say about our theory that perhaps the wrong person was killed accidentally?" Sarah asked when Charles returned from the police station. Sarah, Charles, and Sophie had been stunned by the possibility that Austin might have been the intended victim. After picking at their lunch, they returned to Sarah and Charles' house. Charles left immediately to talk with the detective while Sarah and Sophie waited in the backyard with the dogs.

"We talked about it," Charles reported when he returned. "He said it had occurred to the investigating team, primarily because the poison was found in Austin's dressing room."

"Why would anyone want to kill Austin?" Sarah asked.

"Well, he's famous, and there are lots of sick folks out there. The department briefly thought it could have been a crazy fan, but they talked to his manager and Austin hadn't received any death threats or bizarre communications. And since the nursing home concert was off the grid, never advertised, and only attended by a select group of people, that theory just didn't lead anywhere."

"But if the poison was intended for Austin, the missing roadie comes to mind," Sophie said as she returned from the kitchen with a bowl of water for the dogs. "Maybe he was interested in Angela and thought he had to get Austin out of the way."

"That's possible," Charles responded. "The crew and a couple of the band members thought Hawkins and Angela had a relationship of some kind."

"It would explain why he slipped out the back door so quickly," Sarah reflected. "Have they found him?"

"Not yet …" Charles mumbled offhandedly, seeming to be lost in thought. "There's just something wrong here. Things don't fit. …"

Sarah sent Sophie a nonverbal message to follow her into the house. "We need to let Charles be alone with his thoughts," she said once they were inside. "It's how he works things out."

* * * * *

Charles didn't get to the phone before the machine picked up and the message began. "Hey, Charlie. Halifax here. Give me a …"

"Good morning, Hal," Charles answered as he picked up the phone. He again wondered if it was too late to let Detective Halifax know how much he detested being called Charlie. His old lieutenant, Matt Stokely, had been the last of the old-timers who called him that, and Hal had learned it from Matt. Now that Matt was gone, it seemed that the name could be retired forever. It conjured up too many unpleasant memories of his days on the force. Since his retirement, he'd been Charles to everyone, including his new wife.

Instead, he simply said, "What's up?"

"We identified the guy in that picture you brought us last week."

"Ah. 'Blue suit guy,' as Sophie calls him. Anyone we know?"

"Nope, but he's in the system. Vinny Tuzzo. He did a stretch at Green Haven. Attempted murder for hire charge. He got fifteen years and was out in ten."

"Green Haven, New York?"

"Yeah."

"Why so little time?"

"He gave up the guy who hired him."

"So? Seems like both guys would get more time than that."

"I don't know the details on the plea, but this Tuzzo's a small-time crook who'd been picked up for petty crimes over the years. We think he might have been aiming for the big time by pulling off a professional hit, but, luckily for the intended victim, he failed completely."

"How's that?"

"Some idiot had hired Tuzzo to kill his wife, but fortunately the wife was one tough cookie, and she fought back. According to the reports, she got him in a chokehold and held him until the police got there."

"Strong lady!"

"Prepared lady," the detective clarified. "She taught self-defense to a class of women at the local senior center."

Charles chuckled. "Sounds like something my wife would get into."

As Charles stood and headed for the door, he turned and said, "So what are you doing about this guy, Hal?"

"We're bringing him in, but I've got to be honest with you. We aren't feeling optimistic. I'll let you know what we find."

Chapter 22

"Hey, Charlie. We need you at the station this afternoon. John Hawkins, the roadie guy, is on his way in."

Charles had heard the phone ringing as he and Sarah were approaching the house after walking Barney to the dog park, but he didn't catch it in time.

"Sarah, good news," he said after he erased the message. "They found the missing roadie guy, and Hal wants me to come in this afternoon, probably to sit in on the interrogation."

"That's great news," she responded as she refilled Barney's water bowl and poured glasses of iced tea for herself and Charles. "Is that all he said?"

"That's all he left on the machine. I'll call him and get more details."

That afternoon Charles sat in the viewing room next to the small interrogation room where they were holding John Hawkins, a.k.a. Hawk. Two different teams of interrogators had attempted to get the roadie to change his story, but for three hours the story remained the same. Hawk had been working as part of Austin Bailey's backstage crew for the past year, except when Austin was performing out of the country. "I took care of the equipment and anything else the band needed," he stated.

When asked why he had left suddenly, he dropped his head and mumbled. The detective asked him to speak up. Hawk straightened up and stared straight ahead, avoiding the interviewer's eyes as he told about his short relationship with Angela. He explained that he'd been attracted to her for months but had only recently gotten up the nerve to ask her out. They had gone to the movies the previous week and had a date scheduled for the Saturday following her death. He said the crew teased him about her and said she'd never give him the time of day. His voice cracked when he said, "I was lucky to have the one date."

"So then she refused to see you again? That's when you decided to kill her?"

Hawkins looked shocked and vehemently denied killing her. He seemed to be just then realizing why he was being questioned. "You think I killed her?" he yelled. "I loved her. I was devastated when I heard."

"Is that why you left?"

"I left because I didn't want anyone to see how broken up I was."

"Where have you been?"

"I don't work unless there's a concert. I've been at a buddy's cabin."

"Doing what?"

"Fishin'."

"That doesn't sound like you were too broken up. . . ."

The hours passed with variations of the same questions being asked as the investigators attempted to trip the young man up, but his story never varied and his emotions seemed appropriate to Charles.

"I don't think he did it," he told Hal later.

"Neither do I," the detective admitted, although he had been one of the roughest interrogators.

"You gonna let him go?"

"Yeah, after a while."

"And where does that leave the department?"

"We keep digging, but …"

They continued to sit in the viewing room for a few minutes as yet another investigator entered the interrogation room with a Coke and a sandwich, which he set in front of Hawkins.

"This must be Good Cop?" Charles noted sarcastically.

Hal shook his head conceding defeat. "Let's get some dinner."

They walked up the street to a local deli with a small eat-in area where they ordered Reubens and beer. Neither mentioned the investigation until their sandwiches were gone and they were on their second beers.

"So," Charles began, "what did you learn from Vinny Tuzzo, our blue suit man?"

The detective laughed as he rubbed his forehead. "What a waste of time that turned out to be!"

"How so?"

"The guy was there at his mother's request to accompany her to the concert. At the last minute she decided not to go, but she insisted that he go down and save her a seat in case she changed her mind. Then she called him on his cell several times as she changed her mind back and forth. He was extremely frustrated and ultimately went back up to her room to try to get her to make a decision. That's the point at which your guy snapped the picture."

"Sarah said he tried to leave at one point but was turned back by the cops."

"He told us about that too before we asked. He had decided at one point to just leave but couldn't. I got the idea he was somewhat of a mama's boy. Might be why he wasn't having much success in the world of crime."

* * * * *

"So that's it?" Sophie asked indignantly. "We just stop here and never know who killed Angela?"

"Well, Sophie, look at your cards. They are all on the resolved pile, and there aren't any on the suspects' pile. Of course, that wouldn't be true," Sarah said cautiously, "if you had made a card for Austin."

"What are you saying?" Sophie demanded.

"Whether we like it or not," Sarah replied, "it's looking more and more like the police were right from the beginning. We let our emotions get in the way."

"So you've given up on him," Sophie huffed. Turning to Charles, she pressed, "And you? Are you ready to say Austin Bailey murdered the young woman he had loved like a daughter for twenty-two years?"

"I don't want to say that, Sophie," Charles began, "but …"

"I don't want to talk about this anymore," Sophie declared as she scooped up her 3″ by 5″ cards, grabbed Emma's leash, and marched out the door.

"I'll go get her," Charles offered.

"Let her go," Sarah said with a sigh. "She needs to cool down. I'll take Barney over later."

Chapter 23

"Linda, what are you doing here?" The woman pushed past Sophie, who almost lost her footing.

"What's going on here?" Sophie demanded. She had given Austin's ex-wife her phone number but never expected her to appear at her door. "How did you know where I live?"

"Everything's on the computer," the woman snarled. "I know more than you think I do. Why have you been talking to my neighbors?"

"Linda, sit down so we can talk." As Sophie moved toward the couch, the woman slammed her body into her, causing Sophie to lose her balance and fall against the end table.

"What are you doing?" Sophie gasped as she carefully let herself slide on down to the floor. She reached into her pocket for her cell phone, but the woman kicked it out of her hand.

"Answer me," the woman demanded. "Why are you talking to my neighbors?"

"Linda, I don't understand your anger. When we talked last week, I told you that my friends and I are trying to find Angela's killer in order to clear Austin. Is that what's made you angry?"

"You're trying to prove that I'm the killer! That's why you're talking to my neighbors."

"Wait a minute," Sophie said as she attempted to get up, but the woman pushed her back down with her foot.

"Stay where you are," she ordered. She reached into her pocket and pulled out a small handgun, which she pointed at Sophie's head.

At that moment, Emma came running into the living room and began to growl. The woman turned the gun on the dog and snarled, "Shut that dog up."

Fearing what the woman might do, Sophie called softly to Emma, saying, "It's okay, Emma. Come lie down," and she patted the floor next to her. Emma hesitated, looked at the woman, and cautiously walked over to Sophie and lay on the floor next to her. She continued to produce a low, threatening growl. Sophie rubbed her ear and reassured her for fear that the woman would pull the trigger. The gun was still pointed at Emma.

"Tell me now," the woman demanded. "Why are you snooping around? Are you trying to get me locked up?"

"Linda," Sophie began, "I grew up in your neighborhood. Those are my friends. Why shouldn't I be visiting them?"

"Don't play innocent with me, lady," the woman growled. "I know you were asking questions about me. Are you the one who told the police to pull me in and ask where I was the day that tramp was murdered?"

"Of course not, Linda. I have no connection to the police, but I'm sure you were able to tell them where you were. We both know you didn't kill Angela."

The woman didn't respond, but Sophie saw a look of fear cross her face.

"You do have an alibi, right?" Sophie immediately knew she had said the wrong thing. The gun was now on her.

"What do you think you know?" the woman demanded. Fury filled her eyes and distorted her face. "That girl stole my husband. She took him away from me six years ago, and I wanted him back. It was the only way …"

"You?" Sophie responded with surprise. "You killed Angela?" She suddenly began to understand. "But you told me you left him because of his cruelty. Why would you want him back?"

"How stupid are you anyway?" the woman sneered. "He never laid a hand on me."

"But you said …" Sophie began but stopped abruptly, beginning to realize she'd put her confidence in a mentally deranged woman. "He didn't beat you, did he?"

"Of course not. That sniveling wimp of a man couldn't hurt a flea. He didn't have the guts to stand up and fight, not even with a woman. But he was mine, and she had no right …"

Sophie thought back and realized that Angela would have still been in high school when Austin and Linda separated. "But she was just a child when you separated," Sophie said.

"We didn't *separate*, as you so innocuously put it. He left me. And he left me for that tramp. She deserved what she got."

"You killed her?" Sophie said, even though she knew she was taking her life in her hands. She had to know. "Did you kill her?"

"Shut up," the woman screamed as she kicked Sophie in the side. Sophie fell over in pain. Emma looked at her and then at the woman, but Sophie said, "Stay," in a firm voice.

The woman began to pace. Her distorted face revealed both anger and mounting confusion. She clearly didn't know what to do next.

Sophie wondered what she could do to defuse the situation. She thought about a book she had read back in the 1970s about defending yourself against an attacker. The book had said that people aren't murderers or rapists … they are human beings who do these terrible things, but basically, they are human beings, and you should try to connect with some human emotion they might have.

Sophie continued to lie on the floor thinking, but she knew the silence would only escalate the woman's anger. Finally, she said softly, "I don't know how you were able to get through that. It must have been very painful for you when he left. I know you loved him very much."

The woman didn't respond.

"Tell me about the day he left," she added softly.

The woman remained silent except for a sigh. Sophie hoped that was a good sign.

"Did he tell you why he was leaving?"

"He didn't have the guts to tell me he was leaving." Sophie heard exhaustion in the woman's voice. "I came home from work, and he was gone. The closet was empty."

"What a terrible shock," Sophie said, slowly raising herself up to a sitting position despite the pain.

In a voice barely above a whisper, the woman continued. "I didn't believe it until I saw that all his guitars were gone. If they were gone, so was he." The arm holding the gun was now hanging limply by her side. "I did love him. Maybe it was my fault he left. I don't know. Sometimes I'd get so angry I just couldn't …" she stopped abruptly and looked down at the gun as if seeing it for the first time. She looked at Sophie on the floor and seemed confused. She collapsed onto a nearby chair. Sophie didn't move a muscle.

"We all do the best we can," Sophie finally said softly. "Sometimes we wish it could be better, but we all do the best we can."

Tears began to run down the woman's cheeks. They both remained silent.

The silence was broken by a quick knock on the door, followed by a key in the lock. "Hey, sweetie," Norman called as he closed the door with his back to the living room. When he turned, he saw Sophie on the floor. "What happened?" he cried, rushing to her side.

"I fell. Could you help me up?"

Linda didn't move. The gun lay in her lap. Norman looked over and saw the woman sitting there staring at the floor.

"What ..." he gasped.

Sophie whispered, "It's okay. Let me handle it. Just help me up." Once Sophie was on her feet, she limped over to Linda and gently removed the gun from her lap. Norman started to speak, but she signaled him to remain quiet.

"She needs help, Norman. Would you call 911? Just tell them we have a very sick woman here. Don't mention the gun. We'll deal with that later."

Norman looked reluctant. "Please, Norman," Sophie begged. "I'll call the police as soon as she's safe."

Linda appeared to be catatonic, staring ahead and unresponsive. Tears ran down her face, but she made no effort to wipe them away. Sophie reached for a tissue and wiped the woman's cheeks. "You're going to be okay," she said gently.

Sophie met the paramedics at the door and took them to where Linda sat. They took her vitals and loaded her onto a stretcher. Sophie and Norman followed the ambulance to the hospital, where the examining doctor later told them the woman had apparently had a psychotic break. He asked if she had a history of schizophrenia, and Sophie explained their relationship and gave him Austin's contact information. Sophie and Norman stayed until Linda was admitted to the psychiatric ward for emergency observation.

As they were returning to the lobby, Sarah and Charles rushed in. Sarah hurried to Sophie, and the two women embraced tearfully. Charles and Norman shook hands, and Charles said, "So glad you got to Sophie when you did, buddy."

"Me too," Norman replied. "Is that your cop friend out there?" he asked, leaning over to look out the lobby windows. Two police cars had arrived, and Detective Halifax was heading toward the lobby entrance.

"Yes," Charles responded. "I called Hal and told him to meet us all here. The police should have been there with the paramedics, Norman. What went wrong?"

"Sophie didn't want me to tell the 911 operator about the gun just yet. She was worried about Linda."

"That could have gone very wrong for you folks, but fortunately everyone is safe now," Charles said. "Sorry you have to go through this tonight, Sophie, but Hal will need your statement right away."

"I understand," Sophie replied. "I hope he will understand how sick the woman is," she added.

Detective Halifax called Charles aside to speak with him privately. "Before we get into what happened tonight, I wanted to let you know that I've been on the phone with Elkins PD. They faxed me the domestic disturbance reports from six years ago when the Baileys were still together. It was brutal, but not in the way we assumed. Bailey was taken to the hospital twice with deep cuts. That wife of his could wield a mean butcher knife."

"She was the abuser? Not Austin?"

"Yep. From what the cops said, the guy wouldn't fight back. She was arrested several times, but the guy wouldn't press charges. Calls stopped not long after that. Probably when they separated."

"So, does this mean she lied about being the one who left?"

"He left her." Glancing at the officers who were waiting in the lobby, Halifax added, "We can talk later. I need to get these folks over to the station and get their statements."

"I'd like to sit in," Charles said.

"Of course," Hal replied. "Bring Sarah along with you."

Just then, Austin came rushing into the lobby. "What happened?" he asked anxiously.

Charles gave him an abbreviated version of what had happened and explained that they were on their way to the police station. "You'll need to stay here and talk to the doctor."

"I've probably heard many versions of the story," Austin replied, looking defeated. "This isn't our first late-night trip to the psych ward. Linda and I have been through this many times."

"I don't think you've ever heard this particular ending to the story," Charles responded. Austin didn't know that his ex-wife had confessed to murdering Angela. He learned it an hour later when he joined his friends in Detective Halifax's office.

It was 2:00 a.m. when Charles and Sarah finally left the station. Sophie and Norman were right behind them. Austin stayed behind to talk with the detective.

"Do you think Sophie will be okay alone tonight?" Charles asked.

"I'm sure my friend won't be alone tonight," Sarah replied with a knowing smile.

Chapter 24

"**H**appy birthday," Sarah said cheerfully when her friend answered the phone a few days later.

"Humph," Sophie responded.

"Well, you sure don't sound very cheerful, considering it's your birthday and I was calling to invite you to go out to dinner tonight with Charles and me. We're …"

"Stop right there," Sophie demanded. "The one thing I refuse to do on my seventy-sixth birthday is to be somebody's third wheel."

"No, Sophie, wait a minute. I meant you and Norman, of course. We were thinking …"

"Norman is out of town," Sophie exclaimed, again interrupting her friend. "He had some important business to take care of—obviously more important than my seventy-sixth birthday." Sarah couldn't tell if her friend was angry or hurt. *Probably both*, she thought. *This isn't going well.*

"We want you to go with us, Sophie. Charles is excited about it. He even called ahead and ordered a birthday cake. He wanted it to be a surprise, but I decided you should know. You won't be a third wheel. You're the reason we're going out."

Sophie didn't respond right away, but then with a big sigh, she said, "I guess I could go. Obviously, I don't have any other plans, but I'm not in the best of moods, and I don't want to be a wet blanket on your evening."

"Sophie, you couldn't be a wet blanket if you practiced for a month."

Sophie sighed again. "Tim called to wish me a happy birthday. He said maybe we could get together this weekend. I guess I just made too much of this birthday. Everyone else seems to think it's just another day."

"We'll pick you up at 6:00, okay?"

"Okay," her friend responded with another sigh.

"We've made a big mistake, Charles," Sarah announced as she hung up the phone.

"How's that?"

"Sophie is going to spend her entire birthday sad and feeling rejected. I'm so sorry we decided to do it this way."

"It was Norman's idea," Charles reminded her.

"Yes, but I should have realized how upset she'd be if she thought no one cared."

"She'll be fine when she sees all of her friends and family in the restaurant," Charles responded.

Sometimes men just don't get it, Sarah told herself silently.

Sarah served the bacon and eggs she had prepared for their breakfast and set a small glass of orange juice by each of their plates.

"Turkey bacon?" her husband asked as he took his first bite.

"Yes."

"Egg whites?"

"Yes."

"And this orange juice … were you able to locate an artificial orange grove?"

"You are in almost as bad a mood as Sophie," Sarah announced. "What's going on?"

"It started when I ordered that cake," he grumbled. "I was reminded of all the things I've given up. Eating used to be a joy, and now I feel like I'm just eating to stay alive."

"Well, in a way that's probably exactly what we're doing. I'm preparing the foods that your doctor said will provide the nourishment you need without endangering your heart."

"Don't you think we can spruce it up a bit?"

Sarah was quiet for a moment and then stated, "You may be right. I really haven't put much thought into our meals lately. I saw a book the other day with heart-healthy recipes. How about I go buy it, and then we can go through it together. I'll bet we can come up with some new ideas."

"I'm game. I'll even help you prepare them," Charles offered.

"And in the meantime, I've had an idea about our other problem."

"Other problem?" Charles queried as he spread sugar-free jelly on his toast.

"The party is all arranged, and I have the day free. I think I'll take Sophie somewhere for the day. That will cheer her up."

"Where?"

"Maybe into Hamilton, to the quilt museum."

"Or," Charles said as he reached for the newspaper, "how about the Craft Festival at the Hamilton convention center? That would be something a little different."

"I'll call and ask her," Sarah said eagerly.

"Is this a sympathy outing?" Sophie asked once Sarah explained the plan.

"Well," she thought a moment and said, "I suppose it is. I think you and I need a little cheering up. What do you think?"

"I'm game," Sophie responded, and Sarah could hear the spark returning to her voice. "It sounds like fun. We might even get some ideas for new activities. I've been wanted to do something crafty."

"See you in a half hour?"

"Works for me," Sophie confirmed, sounding like her old self.

* * * * *

"Park over there," Sophie said, pointing toward the handicapped spaces. "I have my tag to put on your windshield." The lot was packed already, and they were lucky to find parking near the door.

As they entered the convention center, Sophie reached for her wallet, but Sarah laid her hand on her friend's arm and said, "Not today, birthday girl," as she passed a few bills to the cashier, who handed them each a ticket and a map showing the locations of all the vendors.

"Wow," Sophie exclaimed as she looked around. "I don't know where to start."

"Let's head over to Aisle 1 and just make our way around until we get tired." But their plan didn't work, because on the way to Aisle 1 they spotted a quilt vendor, and as if pulled by a magnet, they headed straight for the booth.

"Look at these placemats," Sophie said. "They put our club's to shame!"

"Now, Sophie, we could have done ours just as fancy, but we'd only have completed a few rather than the 120 we ended up with. But look at this wall hanging …"

The next few hours were filled with joyful exclamations as the two women excitedly examined and appreciated the creativity shown by the participating artists.

"How do you suppose one gets to bring their crafts to a show like this?" Sophie asked when they finally took a break at the snack bar.

"I read in the article this morning that this is a juried show, so everything is reviewed to be sure it meets the show's high standards. I'm sure they also pay a very high fee to exhibit here."

"Well, they're probably getting their money back. Have you noticed the prices on these things?"

"Yes, but I'm considering a purchase," Sarah responded.

"The mugs?"

"Yes, that pottery really caught my eye. Did you watch the potter working a vase into shape on her wheel?"

"It looked very messy," Sophie replied, "but I loved the result."

Once they were rested they continued exploring, but they soon realized they couldn't see half of what was there. They were both getting tired and took another snack bar break before deciding to head home.

"This has been a great birthday," Sophie announced as they were driving home.

"And it's not finished," Sarah added. "We still have dinner."

"I'm a bit tired, Sarah. I just might skip …"

"No skipping, my friend. Remember Charles' special-order cake?"

"Oh, I almost forgot! Of course, no skipping."

They chatted about the show and their quilting plans as they drove home. As Sophie was getting out of the car in front of her house, Sarah called out, "See you at 6:00," and Sophie waved her agreement.

* * * * *

"Austin called while you were out," Charles announced as they were dressing for the party.

"He's coming, isn't he?" Sarah asked, sounding concerned that he might cancel in light of what was going on with his ex-wife. "It's important that he be there."

"Yes, he's coming. He just wanted to let us know what was going on with Linda since he didn't want to be talking about it tonight."

"And?"

"There was a preliminary hearing, but she was unable to attend. They have her medicated and will be keeping her in the psych ward for a full examination. The judge wants to see their report before he can decide what happens next."

"Will there be a trial?"

"Only if they determine that she is competent to stand trial."

"It's pretty clear she's a very sick woman," Sarah responded. "And Austin said she was diagnosed with schizophrenia years ago."

"True, but there's also the issue of premeditation," Charles explained. "She was able to plan the murder. She bought a nurse's uniform so she could blend in at the nursing home.

She managed to get the poison and find the perfect time to carry out her plan. She was seen there several times before the concert."

"But when she arrived at Sophie's house, she was clearly out of her head."

"True, she is mentally ill, and she certainly had a psychotic break that day at Sophie's, but the prosecutor will be factoring in the fact that she was able to plan and carry out the crime. The legal definition of insanity is not the same as the medical definition."

"Do they actually put mentally ill people in prison?" Sarah asked.

"There are more mentally ill people in prison than in mental hospitals," Charles responded.

"Do they get treatment?"

"Well, it depends on your definition of treatment. They can get psychotropic drugs for their condition. At any rate, Linda will be confined, either in a mental institution or a prison, and she won't be a danger to anyone in the future."

"I'm glad for Austin's sake. He's been through enough."

Chapter 25

They arrived at Sophie's front door at precisely 6:00 p.m., and Charles presented her with an orchid corsage. She was dressed in a long navy blue dress with a lace jacket that she had purchased the previous year for a formal party she attended with Norman. "Oh, Charles, this is beautiful," she cried. "I haven't received a corsage since my high school prom."

"You look pretty enough to be going to a prom," Sarah commented.

"I decided to dress up tonight," Sophie responded. "This is a special occasion."

She doesn't know how special, Sarah thought as she glanced at Charles, who appeared to be thinking the same thing as he pinned the corsage on Sophie's lapel.

When they entered the restaurant fifteen minutes later, a cheer went up, and Sophie grabbed both cheeks in shock. At that moment, the pianist began playing "Happy Birthday," and Sophie's guests joined in. Sarah could tell that Sophie was fighting to hold back the emotion she was feeling.

She couldn't hold back any longer once Norman stepped out of the crowd and took her in his arms. "Happy birthday, my love," he whispered, and Sarah caught the quick movement of her friend wiping away a tear.

Norman led the birthday girl to one of the three long tables that had been prepared for the occasion. She was placed at the head of the middle table and was greeted by her family and her closest friends. As she looked around, she saw that the other two tables were filled with friends from the quilt club and the community. Ruth was there with the entire Running Stitches staff, and Vicky from the volunteer office was sitting with a man she assumed was her husband. Other restaurant customers seated at surrounding tables appeared to be joining in the party spirit.

Waiters began taking their drink orders while other staff members took orders for one of the three Italian dishes that had been prepared especially for the occasion.

"This is probably the first time in my life that I am happier than I am hungry," Sophie announced as she stood to personally greet her guests sitting at the other two tables.

"You look so elegant, Sophie," Ruth said as she and Sophie hugged. "Did you suspect what was happening?"

"Not for a minute," Sophie responded. "I dressed up because I felt I needed to acknowledge the fact that I've been in this world for seventy-six years and that's an accomplishment worth recognizing!"

"You bet it is," several of the quilters agreed.

For the next few hours, Sophie's friends and family ate, drank, laughed, and enjoyed their time together. Sarah didn't think she had ever seen Sophie looking so happy. She especially enjoyed seeing the looks exchanged between her friend and Norman. *They are in love, whether Sophie is willing to admit it or not*, she thought with a smile.

As the evening was ending, Charles stood and clapped to get everyone's attention. "I'd like to introduce a good friend of mine who I'm sure you all know. Austin Bailey, please come up."

Austin stood, and everyone cheered and applauded.

"Thank you," he responded graciously and even a bit timidly. "This is Sophie Ward's night, and I don't want to steal the show, but I'd like to sing my latest song for her."

Everyone applauded.

"I wrote this one night while I was in my hometown. Well, come to think of it," he added, turning toward Sophie, "it's Sophie's hometown too. Anyway, one night I stretched out in the field behind my grandmother's house and stared up at the stars and strummed my guitar to the music that came into my head. That night I was feeling very close to a talented young girl we recently lost, and the words began to flow."

Austin, strumming his guitar, began to sing a soft and tender ballad dedicated to Angela. Everyone tearfully joined in the final chorus.

♪ *You were our little darlin' from the day you were born,*
   Your life just beginning when from us you were torn,
   My heart won't recover from the depth of those scars
   As I sit here reminiscing beneath Missouri stars. ♪

See full quilt on back cover.

PROJECT

BENEATH MISSOURI STARS

Sarah designed this quilt to represent the stars in the sky above Austin's grandparents' farm. Make this 54″ × 72″ quilt and your loved one will be cozy "Beneath Missouri Stars."

MATERIALS

Blocks:

    Light fabric, 1¼ yards

    Medium fabric, 1¼ yards

    Dark fabric, 1¾ yards

Side and corner triangles: Medium fabric, 1½ yards

Sashing: Dark fabric, ½ yards

Backing: 3½ yards

Batting: 62″ × 80″

Binding: 2¼″ wide × ½ yard

> **Tip** ‖ Sarah made the quilt scrappy by using two identical "layer cakes" instead of the light and medium block yardage.

Project Instructions

Seam allowances are ¼".

MAKE A BLOCK

Instructions are for 1 block. Make 18.

Square-in-a-Square Center

1. Cut 1 square 6½" × 6½" from a light fabric.

2. Cut 4 squares 3½" × 3½" from a medium fabric. Draw a diagonal line from corner to corner on the wrong side of each medium square.

3. Align 1 medium square at a corner of the light square, right sides facing. Sew on the diagonal line.

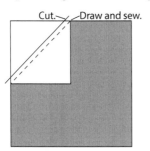

4. Trim through both layers, ¼" away from the sewn line. Press.

5. Repeat for the remaining 3 corners.

QST/HST Units

QST = quarter-square triangle; HST = half-square triangle.

1. Cut 2 squares 4¼″ × 4¼″ from a light fabric.

2. Cut 2 squares 4¼″ × 4¼″ from a medium fabric. Draw a diagonal line from corner to corner on the wrong side of each medium square.

3. Align each light square with a medium square, right sides facing. Sew on *each side* of the diagonal line, ¼″ *away* from the line each time. Cut on the diagonal line to create 4 HST units. Press.

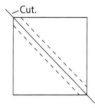

4. Cut each HST unit in half diagonally to create 8 QST units.

5. Cut 4 squares 3⅞″ × 3⅞″ from the dark fabric. Cut each square in half diagonally.

6. Sew together a QST unit and a dark triangle to make a QST/HST unit. Repeat to make 4 with the light fabric on the bottom left and 4 with the light fabric on the bottom right.

7. Sew together 2 QST/HST units. Make 4. *Note the orientation of the units!*

Block Assembly

1. Cut 4 squares 3½″ × 3 ½″ from the dark fabric for the corners.

2. Create 3 rows; sew the rows together.

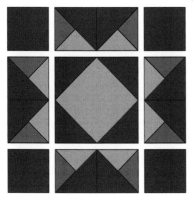

Repeat to make 18 blocks total.

ASSEMBLE AND FINISH THE QUILT

CT = corner triangle; ST = side triangle;
WOF = width of fabric.

1. From the dark fabric, cut 17 strips 1″ × WOF.
Trim and piece together for the sashing:

> 24 strips 1″ × 12½″
> 2 strips 1″ × 13½″
> 2 strips 1″ × 38½″
> 2 strips 1″ × 63½″
> 1 strip 1″ × 76″

2. From the medium fabric:

> Cut 3 squares 19″ × 19″.
> Cut these in half twice diagonally for the STs.

For the STs

> Cut 2 squares 10⅛″ × 10⅛″.
> Cut these in half once diagonally for the CTs.

For the CTs

Tip || This quilt is sewn together in diagonal rows. *IMPORTANT: Refer to the quilt assembly diagram for each step.*

3. Sew together blocks and 1″ × 12½″ sashing strips as shown to create 6 rows. *Do not add the STs yet.*

4. Add sashing strips in the lengths as indicated to the ***top*** of Rows 1, 2, and 3.

5. Add sashing strips in the lengths as indicated to the ***bottom*** of Rows 4, 5, and 6.

6. Add STs to the rows. *Do not add the CTs yet.*

7. Join the rows, adding the remaining sashing strip between Rows 3 and 4.

8. Add the 4 CTs.

9. Layer the pieced top with batting and backing. Quilt and bind as desired.

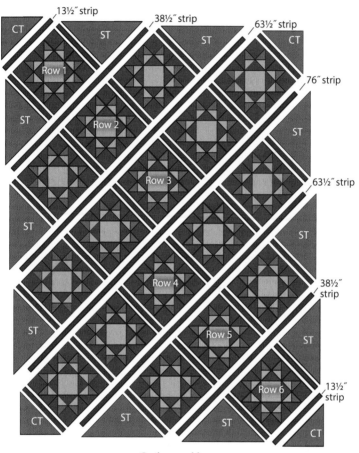

Quilt assembly

READER'S GUIDE:
A QUILTING COZY SERIES
by Carol Dean Jones

1. The Meals on Wheels program provides meals to home-bound people. What other benefits do you think the recipient receives as a result of these visits? What benefits do you think the volunteers receive?

2. Sarah and Sophie stopped at several quilt shops enroute to Elkins. Does this remind you of any serendipitous quilt-shopping opportunities you've had?

3. The band members suggested that Austin may have been having an affair with Angie. Did you suspect that at any point? How would you describe his relationship with the young woman?

4. Sarah and Ruth suspected that Peggy was being abused. Were they right to not intervene? At what point did they become involved? What would you have done?

5. Did you suspect Austin at any point? Did the reports of domestic violence affect your thinking? Who did you think killed the young woman?

6. Once you learned who had committed the murder, what did you think the penalty should have been?

A Note
from the Author

I want to thank my many loyal readers for the hours you have spent reading the books in this series. You have stayed with me for the long haul, following Sarah and her cohorts from the beginning.

I hope these stories have inspired you to find ways to make your own retirement years fulfilling and fun. And if you aren't already a quilter, I hope you'll give quilting (or some other creative outlet) a try.

I love hearing from you and hope you will continue to contact me on my blog or send me an email.

Best wishes,

Carol Dean Jones
caroldeanjones.com
quiltingcozy@gmail.com

A Quilting Cozy Series by Carol Dean Jones

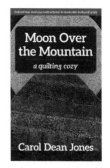